A Voyage to the Moon

Cyrano De Bergerac, Archibald Lovell

La terre me fut importune,
Ie pris mon efsort vers les Cieux,
Iy vis le foleil, et la lune,
Et maintenant Iy vois les Dieux.

CYRANO DE BERGERAC.

("All weary with the earth too soon,
I took my flight into the skies,
Beholding there the sun and moon
Where now the Gods confront my eyes.")

—*From a 17th Century Engraving of the original portrait
by Zacharie Heince.*

DOUBLEDAY and McGUIRE Co

A
VOYAGE
TO THE MOON
BY MONSIEUR
CYRANO DE
BERGERAC

NEW YORK

DOUBLEDAY and McCLURE Co

M. DCCC. XCIX.

CONTENTS.

List of Illustrations.

alas, admit that he was not a Gascon. He ought to have been one, he certainly deserved to be one. But Fortune, who seems to have taken pleasure in always making him just miss his destiny, began by doing him this first and greatest wrong of not letting him be born a Gascon. The family was not even of distant Gascon origin, but was Périgourdin; Bergerac itself is a small town near Périgueux. Cyrano, however, did his best to repair this as well as the other wrongs of Destiny; he acquired the Gascon accent, and often made himself pass for a Gascon.

The fortune of his early education made him fall into the hands of a country curate, who was an insufferable pedant (the species seems to have been common at that time), and who had no real scholarship (the two things are by no means contradictory). Cyrano dubbed his master an " Aristotelic Ass," and wrote to his father that he preferred Paris.

This period of exile had one very im-

portant result, however: the formation
of his first and most lasting friendship,
that with Lebret, who shared in the
instruction of the country curate, but
with a more docile acceptance of his
teachings.   Here again Fortune seems
to have played tricks with Cyrano, in
giving him by accident for life-long
friend one who just missed being what
a real friend should be; who was true
and loyal, but who was always seeking
to reform Cyrano or to push him forward in the world; who admired him,
who loved him, but who was of such
opposite nature that he understood him
not at all.

Back at Paris, Cyrano was sent to the
Collège de Beauvais—afterward Racine's college—where he completed the
course, under the principalship of another pedant named Grangier, who was
a little more scholarly, but no less ridiculous than the first, and who figures
in the leading rôle of Cyrano's comedy
Le Pédant joué.   He lived the Paris
student's life, burning honest trades-

men's signs and "doing other crazy things," as his contemporary Tallemant des Réaux tells us. On leaving college he started upon a downward track, according to Lebret; "on which," says the same good Lebret, "I dare to boast that I stopped him . . . by compelling him to enter the company of the Guards with me." It may be doubted whether a temporary suspension of the paternal allowance had nothing to do with the matter; and whether, after all, Cyrano felt so much repugnance to entering this company of the Guards.

For this company was the famous regiment of the "garde-nobles," commanded by Carbon de Castel-Jaloux, a "triple Gascon" and a "triple brave." And his men were hardly a step behind him, all of them nobles—that was an essential condition of entrance—and almost all of them Gascons. Cyrano, at first in the position rather of the Christian than of the Cyrano of M. Rostand's play, by his gallantry and wit compelled them to accept him, and even won among these "braves" the title of "*démon de la bravoure*." Unable to be the most Gascon of the Gascons, he made it up by being more Gascon than the Gascons.

Among his exploits the most famous is that of the fight with the hundred ruffians; for this appears to be not a dramatic creation or a legend, but history. One of his poet-friends, Linière (the name is sometimes spelt Lignière) a writer of epigram and contributor to the "Recueils" or "Keepsakes" of the epoch, had wounded the susceptibilities of a certain "grand seigneur," who planned to avenge himself by the same method which another noble lord, in the eighteenth century, actually used against Voltaire. He posted his hundred men at the Porte de Nesle, to waylay Linière. Linière, hearing of it, came to take refuge with Cyrano for the night. But Cyrano would not receive him. " No, you shall sleep at home," said he. " Here, take

this lantern" (this is M. Brun's ver-
sion), "walk behind me and hold the
light, and I'll make bed-quilts of them
for you!"   And the next morning
there were found scattered about the
Porte de Nesle two dead men, seven
wounded, and many hats, sticks, and
pikes.

According to Lebret's account, the
battle took place in broad daylight, and
had several witnesses.   For the rest,
his story coincides with that above.
And all versions agree in saying that
M. de Cuigy and M. de Brissailles—
both men of the time fairly well known:
one the son of an Advocate of the Parliament of Paris, the other Mestre de
Camp of the Prince de Conti's regiment—bore witness to the facts; and
that the story became generally known,
and was never denied.   Perhaps it will
not be well to guarantee the exactness
of the number one hundred; but the
story must be for the most part true.

Another exploit, less magnificent, but
perhaps as characteristic of the wild

temper of Cyrano, is his battle with
Fagotin. A mountebank named Brioché had a theatre of marionnettes, near
the Pont-Neuf, and used an ape called
Fagotin, fantastically dressed, to attract spectators. Some enemy of Cyrano, perhaps Dassoucy, one day persuaded Brioché to dress his ape up in
imitation of Cyrano, with long sword
and nose as long. Cyrano, arriving
and seeing this parody of himself exalted on a platform, unsheathes in blind
rage, drives the crowd of lackeys and
loafers right and left with the flat of
his sword, and impales the poor ape
who was holding out his sword in a
posture of self-defence. According to
the contemporary pamphlet, partly in
prose and partly in verse, which was
made upon this marvellous adventure,
Brioché brought suit for damages
against Bergerac. But even in these
ridiculous circumstances Cyrano man-
aged to get the laughers on his side; and
claiming that in the country of art there
was no such thing as gold and silver, and

that he had a right to pay in the money of the country, he promised to eternize the dead ape in Apollinic verse; and so was acquitted.

The story of Montfleury, the fat actor whom Cyrano detested, is hardly less fantastic; and in connection with it we have the witness of Cyrano's own letter " Against Montfleury the Fat, bad Actor and bad Author," the tenth of the *Satiric Letters*. According to all the books of theatrical anecdotes, Cyrano one evening ordered him off the stage, and forbade him to reappear for a month; and when two days later he did reappear, Cyrano once more drove him in disgrace to the wings. The audience protesting, Cyrano challenged them each and all to meet him in duel, and carried his point. Whether he offered to take down their names in order or not, does not appear.

In the meantime, more serious work turned up. The regiment of the cadets was sent against the Germans, entered Mouzon, was besieged there. In

a sortie, Cyrano was seriously wounded,
a musket-ball passing through his body.
Hardly recovered from his wound, he
rejoined the army at the siege of Arras,
in 1640; unfortunately for the story, he
was probably no longer with the cadets
there, but in the regiment of the Prince
de Conti. Again he was wounded, this
time even more seriously, with a sword-
cut in the throat. And compelled to
abandon the military career, he returned to Paris and took up his studies
and his writing.

For he had always been a student
and a poet. It is probable that the
Pédant joué was in part composed during his college days. Lebret pictures
him to us as studying between two
duels, and working at an Elegy in all
the noise of the regimental barracks,
" as undistractedly as if he had been in
a quiet study." He now joined a group
of independents in thought and life,
naturalists in ethics and empiricists in
philosophy, and forced his way into a
private class of the philosopher Gas-

sendi, where he had for fellow-students Hesnaut, Chapelle, Bernier, and almost certainly a young Jean-Baptiste Poquelin, who was very soon to take the name of Molière, found the "Illustre Théâtre," and after its failure start on a fifteen years' tour of the provinces.

Cyrano was an earnest and capable student of philosophy, and came to it with the fresh interest not only of his own personality, but of a young man of barely twenty-two; he naturally imposed himself as a sort of leader in the group of young "libertins" or freethinkers, just as he had done among the Guards.   He knew well not only Gassendi, but also Campanella, and of course Descartes, in his works at least. He even seems to have read widely among the half-philosophers, half-occultists of the fifteenth and early sixteenth centuries, such as Cornelius Agrippa, Jerome Cardan, Abbot Tritheim, César de Nostradamus, etc.   Among the ancients, his first favorites were Lucretius and Pyrrho: Pyrrho whom he es-

pecially admired, "because he was so
nobly free, that no thinker of his age
had been able to enslave his opinions;
and so modest, that he would never
give final decision on any point."
There is much of Cyrano in this phrase,
both in the half-bold modesty and in the
half-timid fierceness of independence.
Cyrano shuddered at the thought of
having even a single one of his ideas
enslaved to those of another thinker.
Just as he had refused the Maréchal de
Gassion for patron when he was in the
Guards, so he would accept no one's
magister dixit, no patron of his thought,
not even the Aristotle of the Schools.

The period of his life from 1643 to
1653 is a very obscure one. Yet probably almost all of his works were composed during this time. He may have
travelled; there are traditions and sug-
gestions that he visited England, Italy,
even Poland. He probably stood in
danger of persecution from the Jesuits
on account of his philosophical ideas,
and may have suffered it, as did his

contemporaries Campanella and Galileo, or, to mention a French poet only a little older than he, *Théophile de Viau*, who was even condemned to death for less independence than Cyrano's; though the sentence was fortunately commuted. He probably mingled somewhat in the society of the "Précieuses" of the time as well as in that of the "libertins"; for he has left a series of "Love-Letters" which must almost exactly have suited the taste of those who prepared Discourses on the Tender Passion. He probably had many duels still, for Lebret tells us that he served a hundred times as second—the round number is to be taken as such—and any one acquainted with the epoch, or with the *Three Musketeers* of Dumas, knows that the seconds fought as well as the principals. Lebret adds, to be sure, that he never had a quarrel on his own account, but we may perhaps take this as a bit of the conscientious "white-washing" which Lebret could not refrain from in speaking of his friend's reputation; for we know enough of his character even from Lebret, and of his life from other sources, to make a gentle peacefulness, so out of keeping with the epoch, somewhat doubtful; and then—there was his nose.

The Nose is authentic also. It appears in all the portraits, of which there are four. And in all of these it is the same: not a little ugly nose, flat at the top and projecting at the bottom in a little long gable turned up at the end; but a large, generous, well-shaped nose, hooked rather than retroussé, and planted squarely in the symmetrical middle of the face; not ridiculous, but monumental! The anecdotes of the duels it caused are so many, that one comes in spite of oneself to believe some of them. It is said that this nose brought death upon more than ten persons; that one could not look upon it, but he must unsheathe; if one looked away, it was worse; and as for speaking of Noses, that was a subject which Cyrano reserved for himself, to do it fitting honor. Listen to his treatment of it in the *Pédant joué :* "This veridic nose arrives everywhere a quarter of an hour before its master. Ten shoemakers, good round fat ones too, go and sit down to work under it out of the rain." As for defending large noses, as the index of valor, intelligence, and all high qualities, it will appear in the *Voyage to the Moon* that he could do it as well with his pen as with his sword.

The end of his life was difficult and sad. He was finally compelled to accept the patronage of the Duc d'Arpajon, for no man could live or even exist by literature at that period, except as literature brought patronage or pensions. The great Corneille himself, than whom no one could be more simply sturdy and high of character, wrote begging letters to the great minister who controlled the pensions of literature. Cyrano dedicated the edition of his "Miscellaneous Works" in 1654 to the Duc d'Arpajon, in an epistle which fulfils, but with dignity and independence, the laws of the *genre*, and accompanied it with a sonnet addressed to the Duke's daughter, which is in the taste of the time, yet considerably better than the taste of the time. Things went well till *Agrippine* appeared, which had a "succès de scandale"; but its "belles impiétés," as the happy book-seller called them, seem to have pleased the timidly orthodox Duke less. In the meantime Cyrano had received a wound from a falling beam—whether by mere accident or not, will never be known; but Cyrano had many enemies, and it has generally been thought that there was purpose behind the accident. For whatever reason, the Duc d'Arpajon seems to have advised Cyrano to leave him, and Cyrano was received by Regnault des Bois-Clairs, a friend of Lebret. There he was kindly cared for —and lectured on the evil of his past life—by Lebret and three women of the Convent of the Daughters of the Cross: Sœur Hyacinthe, an aunt of

Cyrano himself; Mère Marguerite, the superior of the convent; and the Baronne de Neuvillette, a cousin of Cyrano, who was Madeleine Robineau, and had married the Baron Christophe de Neuvillette, killed at the siege of Arras in 1640. The three women persuaded themselves that they had converted Cyrano to the true Church. This is doubtful, since he dragged himself away to the country to die, at the house of the cousin whom he speaks of at the end of the *Voyage to the Moon.* In any case, Mére Marguerite reclaimed his body, and he was buried in holy ground at the convent.

The Voyage to the Moon was not published till 1656, the year after Cyrano's death. It was certainly written as early as 1650, probably in 1649. It had been circulated widely in manuscript, and possibly a few copies had been printed, before the author's death. The *Voyage to the Sun*, or, to give the title more accurately, the "Comic History of the States and Empires of the Sun," was probably written immediately after the *Voyage to the Moon*, but was not published till 1662. The *History of the Spark* has never been found, unless that be the sub-title of a part of the *Voyage to the Sun*, as seems fairly probable.

The *Letters* of Cyrano are, in part at least, his earliest work. They were probably scattered over a considerable period in point of composition, but most of them were published in 1654. It is to be remembered that like all the letters of that epoch which we have, they were meant to be read in company, in the *salons*, or sometimes (like that "Against Dassoucy"), in the taverns, corresponding to the modern cafés, where men of letters gathered. They were written not for the postman, but for the parlor; and not so much for the parlor as for the printer. But even with the artificiality of this method, and with the burlesque or précieuse expression that was obligatory in Letters at that time, there are touches of

real sincerity and passion constantly
breaking through.

The *Pédant joué* is a prose-comedy
in five acts, made almost entirely on the
model of the Italian "commedia dell'
arte," a form in which Molière's early
work is written, and which was practi-
cally the only form known at the time
when Cyrano wrote—for the play is
certainly anterior to Corneille's *Men-
teur*. We have the almost obligatory
two pairs of young lovers; the old father who is tyrannical but easily de-
ceived—in this particular case combined
with the pedant-doctor type; the valet
who does the deceiving, in the service
of the young lovers; and the terrible
captain, who takes flight at the shadow
of danger. Cyrano has, however, in-
troduced one new type—a peasant with
his dialect and local characteristics: a
type that Molière used to great advantage later, but hardly so very much better than Cyrano uses it here; witness
the fact that a number of this peasant's
phrases have become proverbs. The

famous scene of "qu'allait-il faire dans
cette galère" (despairingly repeated by
the father who is compelled to give up
his cherished money for the ransom of
a son held in captivity—supposedly—
on a Turkish galley) is exceedingly well
imagined, and Molière did well to use
it, sixteen years after Cyrano's death,
for the two best scenes of his *Fourberies
de Scapin*. It is not a matter to re-
proach Molière with, but it is a case in
which Cyrano should receive due credit.

The only serious poetical work of
Cyrano is his tragedy of *Agrippine,
veuve de Germanicus*, written at some
time in the forties, played in 1653, and
published in 1654. The statement,
repeated categorically by Mr. Sidney
Lee in his recent Life of Shakespeare,
that "Cyrano de Bergerac plagiarized
' Cymbeline,' ' Hamlet,' and ' The Mer-
chant of Venice ' in his 'Agrippina,' "
has not the slightest foundation. There
are no resemblances, either superficial
or essential, on which to base it, and it
is altogether improbable that Cyrano

even knew of Shakespeare's existence. The subject of *Agrippine* is similar to that of Corneille's *Cinna*—a conspiracy under the Roman Empire. There are no resemblances to Corneille's work in the details of the plot, but in general spirit the play is what we call Cornelian, partly because Corneille was the only one who possessed this spirit of the epoch with sufficient creative and individual power to compel the attention of posterity. Cyrano, once more, just missed this. But his play is worthy not only to be ranked with the best dramas of any of his contemporaries except Corneille, but even to be at least compared with Corneille's better work (except perhaps the *Cid* and *Polyeucte*). The play is not thoroughly well constructed, and so misses something of dramatic effectiveness, though by no means missing it entirely; but it is as well constructed as Corneille's *Cinna*, and better than his *Horace*—to take examples only among his greatest plays. It has no scene to compare with that of the clemency of Augustus in *Cinna*, no character-study so fine as that of the different sentiments of Augustus. But it approaches, though it does not quite attain, the heroics of *Horace.* It is full of exaggeration—so is Corneille; and of an exaggeration that sometimes becomes burlesque—as in Corneille; but it is an exaggeration that is high and heroic, like Corneille's. And the high and heroic sometimes—as in a line like this:

Et puis, mourir n'est rien; c'est achever de naitre—

sometimes, but too rarely, drops its exaggeration to become simple — as simple as real heroism, which is the simplest thing in the world.

Except real genius. Real genius is, finally, the essential thing, which Cyrano once more just missed attaining —missed just by the lack of that simplicity, perhaps. But exaggeration, sometimes carried to the burlesque, is the essential trait which makes him what he is; and we cannot wish it away.

CURTIS HIDDEN PAGE.

NOTE ON THE TRANSLATION.

There have been at least three translations into English of the *Voyage to the Moon :* that alluded to on page 1; the present translation; and one made in the eighteenth century by Samuel Derrick. The last is dedicated to the Earl of Orrery, author of " Remarks on the Life and Writings of Jonathan Swift," and attributes its " call from obscurity " to " your Lordship' s mentioning it in your *Life of Swift*" as having served for inspiration to *Gulliver's Travels.*

Samuel Derrick's translation, however, is not so good as that of A. Lovell. The seventeenth century translation is more flowery and fanciful, and by that very fact closer to the original. For though the *Voyage to the Moon* is the most sober in style of Cyrano's works, yet there are still many touches of the " high fantastical " in its manner as well as in its substance. The eighteenth century translator has toned down the style to make it more acceptable to that age of reason and regularity. It is still another case of the irony of Fate pursuing Cyrano; the regularists of seventeenth century literature in France, against whom he struggled so swashbucklerly, had completely triumphed and spread their influence over Europe; so that even in the land where liberty and individuality are native, his work had to suffer correction in all its most fanciful passages. There are constant omissions of phrases or sentences in the eighteenth century translation, and there are also numerous mistakes, as well as many points missed. The seventeenth century translation, on the other hand, is faithful throughout to its original, and accurate as well as vivid.

The translation has been compared throughout with the French of the edition of 1661, and the two or three slight corrections needed have been made in foot-notes. Except for the breaking up of some very long paragraphs, and slight changes in punctuation when necessary for clearness, the text has been reprinted as exactly as possible. All changes or additions, except the correction of evident misprints, have been bracketed.

C. H. P.

A VOYAGE TO THE MOON.

THE
TRANSLATOR
TO THE
READER.

It is now Seven and Twenty Years,
since the Moon appeared first Histori-
cally on the English Horizon:[1] And let
it not seem strange, that she should
have retained Light and Brightness so
long here, without Renovation; when

[1] This evidently refers to an earlier translation
of the *Voyage to the Moon*, published probably in
1660. The present editor will be greatly obliged to
any one who will put him on the track of a copy of
this, or any other early translation from Cyrano,
such as the " Satyrical Characters and handsome
Descriptions, in Letters, written to several Persons
of Quality, by Monsieur De Cyrano Bergerac.
Translated from the French, by a Person of Honor.
London, 1658."

I

we find by Experience, that in the Heavens, she never fails once a Month to change and shift her Splendor. For it is the Excellency of Art, to represent Nature even in her absence; and this being a Piece done to the Life, by one that had the advantage of the true Light, as well as the Skill of Drawing, in this kind, to Perfection; he left so good an Original, which was so well Copied by another Hand, that the Picture might have served for many Years more, to have given the Lovers of the Moon, a sight of their Mistress, even in the darkest Nights; and when she was retired to put on a clean Smock in Phœbus his Apartment; if they had been so curious, as to have encouraged the Exposers.

However, Reader, you have now a second View of her, and that under the same Cover with the Sun too, which is very rare; since these two were never seen before in Conjunction. Yet I would have none be afraid, that their Eyes being dazled with the glorious

Light of the Sun, they should not see her; for Fancy will supply the Weakness of the Organ, and Imagination, by the help of this Mirrour, will not fail to discover them both; though Cynthia lye hid under Apollo's shining Mantle. And so much for the Luminaries.

Now as to the Worlds, which, with Analogy to ours below, I may call the Old and New; that of the Moon having been discovered, tho imperfectly, by others, but the Sun owing its Discovery wholly to our Author:[1] I make no

[1] Among the "others" who had previously "discovered" the Moon, Ariosto is the most prominent. In his *Orlando Furioso*, Astolfo goes to the moon, visits the "Valley of Lost Things," finds there many broken resolutions, idlers' days, lovers' tears, and other such matters; and finally recovers Orlando's lost wits, which he brings back to the earth.

The *Satire Ménippée* (1594) gives, in its *Supplement*, "News from the Regions of the Moon."

Quevedo, the Spanish satirist and novelist (1580–1645), with whose works Cyrano was acquainted, also gives an account of the moon in his *Sixth Vision*.

In England, the Rev. John Wilkins (1614–1672), once Principal of Trinity College, Cambridge, and later Bishop of Chester, a brother-in-law of Crom-

doubt, but the Ingenious Reader will find in both, so extraordinary and surprizing Rarities, as well Natural, Moral, as Civil; that if he be not as yet sufficiently disgusted with this lower World, (which I am sure some are) to think of making a Voyage

well, and one of the founders of the Royal Society, published in 1638 the "*Discovery of a New World; or, a Discourse to prove it is probable there may be another habitable world in the Moon; with a discourse concerning *the possibility of a passage thither*"; and later, in 1640, the "*Discourse* concerning a new Planet; tending to prove it is probable our earth is one of the Planets." These two works are said to have done more than any others to popularize the Copernican system in England. The *Discovery of a New World* was translated into French by Jean de Montagne, and published at Rouen in 1655 or 1656. See Charles Nodier, *Mélanges extraits d'une petite bibliothèque.*

Finally, the most important of Cyrano's predecessors in the discovery of the moon was Francis Godwin, M.A., D.D., Bishop of Llandaff and later of Hereford (1562-1633). It was not till 1638, after the worthy Bishop's death, and in the same year that Rev. (later Bishop) John Wilkins' *Discovery of a New World* was published, that there appeared his "*Man in the Moone; or a Discourse of a Voyage Thither, by Domingo Gonsales, the Speedy Messenger." This was translated into French by Jean Baudoin or Baudouin in 1648, as "L'homme

thither, as our Author has done; he will at least be pleased with his Relations. Nevertheless, since this Age produces a great many bold Wits, that shoot even beyond the Moon, and cannot endure, (no more than our Author) to be stinted by Magisterial Authority, and to believe nothing but what Gray-headed Antiquity gives them leave: It's pity some soaring Virtuoso, instead of Travelling into France, does not take a flight up to the Sun; and by new Observations supply the defects of its History; occasioned not by the Negligence of our Witty French Author, but by the accursed Plagiary of some rude Hand, that in his Sickness, rifted his Trunks, and stole his Papers, as he himself complains.[1]

dans la lune . . . voyage . . . fait par Dominique Gonzalès, aventurier espagnol," and was well known to Cyrano, as we shall see.

In saying that " the sun owes its discovery wholly to our author," the translator appears to be ignorant of a work which Cyrano certainly knew: the *Civitas solis* of Campanella, published in 1623 as a part of his *Realis Philosophiæ Epilogisticæ Partes IV.*

[1] *Cf.* the last sentence of the *Voyage to the Moon.*

Let some venturous Undertaker auspiciously attempt it then; and if neither of the two Universities, Gresham-Colledge, nor Greenwich-Observatory can furnish him with an Instrument of Conveyance; let him try his own Invention, or make use of our Author's Machine: For our Loss is, indeed, so great, that one would think, none but the declared Enemy of Mankind, would have had the Malice, to purloyn and stiffle those rare Discoveries, which our Author made in the Province of the Solar Philosophers; and which undoubtedly would have gone far, as to the settleing our Sublunary Philosophy, which, as well as Religion, is lamentably rent by Sects and Whimseys; and have convinced us, perhaps, that in our present Doubts and Perplexities, a little more, or a little less of either, would better serve our Turns, and more content our Minds.

THE
COMICAL HISTORY

OF THE

STATES AND EMPIRES

OF THE

WORLD

OF THE

MOON.

Written in French by
CYRANO BERGERAC.

And now Englished by
A. LOVELL. A.M.

———

LONDON,
Printed for *Henry Rhodes*, next door to the *Swan-Tavern*, near *Bride-Lane* in *Fleet-Street*, 1687.

[THE TITLE-PAGE OF LOVELL'S TRANSLATION.]

COMICAL HISTORY

OF THE

STATES

AND

EMPIRES

OF THE

WORLD

OF THE

MOON.

CHAPTER I.

Of how the Voyage was Conceived.

I Had been with some Friends at
Clamard, a House near Paris, and
magnificently Entertain'd there by
Monsieur de Cuigy,[1] the Lord of it;

[1] Monsieur de Cuigy, who is mentioned by Lebret
as a friend and admirer of Cyrano, and who was

when upon our return home, about
Nine of the Clock at Night, the Air
serene, and the Moon in the Full, the
Contemplation of that bright Lumi-
nary furnished us with such variety
of Thoughts as made the way seem
shorter than, indeed, it was. Our
Eyes being fixed upon that stately
Planet, every one spoke what he thought
of it: One would needs have it be a
Garret Window of Heaven; another
presently affirmed, That it was the Pan
whereupon *Diana* smoothed *Apollo's*
Bands; whilst another was of Opinion,
That it might very well be the Sun
himself, who putting his Locks up
under his Cap at Night, peeped through
a hole to observe what was doing in
the World during his absence.

"And for my part, Gentlemen," said
I, "that I may put in for a share, and
guess with the rest; not to amuse my

one of the witnesses of his famous battle against
the hundred ruffians, possessed an estate at
Clamart-sous-Meudon, near Paris. He appears as
a character in M. Rostand's play of *Cyrano de
Bergerac.*

self with those curious Notions wherewith you tickle and spur on slow-paced
Time; I believe, that the Moon is a
World like ours, to which this of ours
serves likewise for a Moon."

This was received with the general
Laughter of the Company. "And perhaps," said I, " (Gentlemen) just so they
laugh now in the Moon, at some who
maintain, That this Globe, where we
are, is a World." But I'd as good have
said nothing, as have alledged to them,
That a great many Learned Men had
been of the same Opinion; for that
only made them laugh the faster.

However, this thought, which because of its boldness suted my Humor,
being confirmed by Contradiction, sunk
so deep into my mind, that during
the rest of the way I was big with
Definitions of the Moon which I could
not be delivered of: Insomuch that by
striving to verifie this Comical Fancy
by Reasons of appearing weight, I had
almost perswaded my self already of
the truth on't; when a Miracle, Ac-

cident, Providence, Fortune, or what, perhaps, some may call Vision, others Fiction, Whimsey, or (if you will) Folly, furnished me with an occasion that engaged me into this Discourse. Being come home, I went up into my Closet, where I found a Book open upon the Table, which I had not put there. It was a piece of *Cardanus* [1]; and though I had no design to read in it, yet I fell at first sight, as by force, exactly upon a Passage of that Philosopher where he tells us, That Studying one evening by Candle-light, he perceived Two tall old Men enter in through the door that was shut, who after many questions that he put to them, made him answer, That they were Inhabitants of the Moon, and thereupon immediately disappeared.

[1] Jerome Cardan, 1501-1576, natural philosopher, doctor, astrologer, mathematician, and a voluminous author; in short, a sort of Italian Paracelsus, both by his universal learning, and by his intense interest in all domains of possible knowledge, in which he included astrology and necromancy. His most important work is the one referred to here, the *De Subtilitate Rerum*, 1551.

CYRANO *en route* FOR THE MOON.

—*From a 17th Century Engraving.*

I was so surprised, not only to see a Book get thither of it self; but also because of the nicking of the Time so patly, and of the Page at which it lay upon, that I looked upon that Concatenation of Accidents as a Revelation, discovering to Mortals that the Moon is a World. "How!" said I to my self, having just now talked of a thing, can a Book, which perhaps is the only Book in the World that treats of that matter so particularly, fly down from the Shelf upon my Table; become capable of Reason, in opening so exactly at the place of so strange an adventure; force my Eyes in a manner to look upon it, and then to suggest to my fancy the Reflexions, and to my Will the Designs which I hatch.

"Without doubt," continued I, "the Two old Men, who appeared to that famous Philosopher, are the very same who have taken down my Book and opened it at that Page, to save themselves the labour of making to me the Harangue which they made to *Cardan*.

But," added I, " I cannot be resolved of this Doubt, unless I mount up thither."

" And why not? " said I instantly to my self. " *Prometheus* heretofore went up to Heaven, and stole fire from thence.   Have not I as much Boldness as he?   And why should not I, then, expect as favourable a Success?"

CHAPTER II.

Of how the Author set out, and where he first arrived.

After these sudden starts of Imagination, which may be termed, perhaps, the Ravings of a violent Feaver, I began to conceive some hopes of succeeding in so fair a Voyage: Insomuch that to take my measures aright, I shut my self up in a solitary Country-house; where having flattered my fancy with some means, proportionated to my design, at length I set out for Heaven in this manner.

I planted my self in the middle of a great many Glasses full of Dew, tied fast about me;[1] upon which the Sun so violently darted his Rays, that the Heat, which attracted them, as it does

[1] *Cf.* M. Rostand's *Cyrano de Bergerac*, act III., scene xi.: "One way was to stand naked in the

the thickest Clouds, carried me up so high, that at length I found my self above the middle Region of the Air. But seeing that Attraction hurried me up with so much rapidity that instead of drawing near the Moon, as I intended, she seem'd to me to be more distant than at my first setting out; I broke several of my Vials, until I found my weight exceed the force of the Attraction, and that I began to descend again towards the Earth. I was not mistaken in my opinion, for some time after I fell to the ground again; and to reckon from the hour that I set out at, it must then have been about midnight. Nevertheless I found the Sun to be in the Meridian, and that it was Noon. I leave it to you to judge, in what Amazement I was; The truth is, I was so strangely surprised, that not knowing what to think of that Miracle, I had the

sunshine, in a harness thickly studded with glass phials, each filled with morning dew. The sun in drawing up the dew, you see, could not have helped drawing me up too!" (Miss Gertrude Hall's translation.)

insolence to imagine that in favour of my Boldness God had once more nailed the Sun to the Firmament, to light so generous[1] an Enterprise. That which encreased my Astonishment was, That I knew not the Country where I was; it seemed to me, that having mounted straight up, I should have fallen down again in the same place I parted from.

However, in the Equipage I was in, I directed my course towards a kind of Cottage, where I perceived some smoke; and I was not above a Pistol-shot from it, when I saw my self environed by a great number of People, stark naked: They seemed to be exceedingly surprised at the sight of me; for I was the first, (as I think) that they had ever seen clad in Bottles. Nay, and to baffle all the Interpretations that they could put upon that Equipage, they perceived that I hardly touched the ground as I

[1] Generous = *noble*. *Cf.* Lord Burleigh, *Precepts to his Son :* "Let her not be poor, how *generous* soever; for a man can buy nothing in the market with gentility."

2

walked; for, indeed, they understood
not that upon the least agitation I gave
my Body the Heat of the beams of the
Noon-Sun raised me up with my Dew;
and that if I had had Vials enough
about me, it would possibly have carried me up into the Air in their view.
I had a mind to have spoken to them;
but as if Fear had changed them into
Birds, immediately I lost sight of them
in an adjoyning Forest.   However, I
catched hold of one, whose Legs had,
without doubt, betrayed his Heart.   I
asked him, but with a great deal of pain,
(for I was quite choked) how far they
reckoned from thence to *Paris?*   How
long Men had gone naked in *France?*
and why they fled from me in so great
Consternation?   The Man I spoke to
was an old tawny Fellow, who presently
fell at my Feet, and with lifted-up
Hands joyned behind his Head, opened
his Mouth and shut his Eyes: He
mumbled a long while between his
Teeth, but I could not distinguish an
articulate Word; so that I took his

Language for the maffling[1] noise of a Dumb-man.

Some time after, I saw a Company of Souldiers marching, with Drums beating; and I perceived Two detached from the rest, to come and take speech of me. When they were come within hearing, I asked them, Where I was? "You are in *France*," answered they: "But what Devil hath put you into that Dress? And how comes it that we know you not? Is the Fleet then arrived? Are you going to carry the News of it to the Governor? And why have you divided your Brandy into so many Bottles?" To all this I made answer, That the Devil had not put me into that Dress: That they knew me not; because they could not know all Men: That I knew nothing of the *Seine's* carrying Ships to *Paris:* That I had no news for the *Marshal de l' Hospital;*[2] and that I was not loaded with

---

[1] Stammering, mumbling; a North of England word.

[2] Paul Lacroix, the editor of the French edition of Cyrano's works, not understanding this phrase,

Brandy. "Ho, ho," said they to me, taking me by the Arm, "you are a merry Fellow indeed; come, the Governor will make a shift to know you, no doubt on't."

They led me to their Company, where I learnt that I was in reality in *France*, but that it was in *New-France:* So that some time after, I was presented before the Governor, who asked me my Country, my Name and Quality; and after that I had satisfied him in all Points, and told him the pleasant Success of my Voyage, whether he believed it, or only pretended to do so, he had the goodness to order me a Chamber in his Apartment.   I was very happy, in

has ingeniously invented the interpretation of "quarantine officer" for it. Not only have the words never had this meaning, but they are evidently a proper name. And in fact *François de l'Hospital, Maréchal de France*, was Governor of Paris in 1649, the year when the *Voyage to the Moon* was probably written. Cyrano, thinking he has fallen in France, near Paris, and being asked if he carries news of the fleet to the Governor, naturally answers that he knows nothing of ships going to Paris, and that he carries no news to the Maréchal de l'Hospital.

meeting with a Man capable of lofty
Opinions, and who was not at all surprised when I told him that the Earth
must needs have turned during my
Elevation; seeing that having begun to
mount about Two Leagues from *Paris*,
I was fallen, as it were, by a perpen-
dicular Line in *Canada*.

CHAPTER III.

Of his Conversation with the Vice-Roy of New France; and of the system of this Universe.

When I was going to Bed at night, he came into my Chamber, and spoke to me to this purpose: "I should not have come to disturb your Rest, had I not thought that one who hath found out the secret of Travelling so far in Twelve hours space, had likewise a charm against Lassitude. But you know not," added he, "what a pleasant Quarrel I have just now had with our Fathers, upon your account? They'll have you absolutely to be a Magician; and the greatest favour you can expect from them, is to be reckoned only an Impostor: The truth is, that Motion which you attribute to the Earth [1] is a

[1] In connection with this discussion it is to be remembered that nearly two centuries were re-

pretty nice Paradox; and for my part I'll frankly tell you, That that which hinders me from being of your Opinion, is, That though you parted yesterday from *Paris*, yet you might have arrived today in this Country without the Earth's turning: For the Sun having drawn you up by the means of your Bottles, ought he not to have brought you hither; since according to *Ptolemy*, and the Modern Philosophers,[1] he marches obliquely, as you make the Earth to move? And besides, what great Probability have you to imagine, that the Sun is immoveable, when we see it go? And

quired for the Copernican system, promulgated in 1543, in the *De orbium cælestium revolutionibus*, to become generally popularized; and that in 1633, only sixteen years before the *Voyage to the Moon* was written, Galileo had been compelled by the Inquisition to deny the motion of the earth.

[1] According to the Ptolemaic system, still generally accepted by "modern Philosophers" at the time of Cyrano's writing, the fixed stars, the sun, the moon, and each of the five (then known) planets, revolved about the earth in different orbits, according to various "epicycles" and "excentrics."

what appearance is there, that the Earth turns with so great Rapidity, when we feel it firm under our Feet?"

"Sir," replied I to him, "These are, in a manner, the Reasons that oblige us to think so: In the first place, it is consonant to common Sense to think that the Sun is placed in the Center of the Universe; seeing all Bodies in nature standing in need of that radical Heat, it is fit he should reside in the heart of the Kingdom, that he may be in a condition readily to supply the Necessities of every Part; and that the Cause of Generations should be placed in the middle of all Bodies, that it may act there with greater Equality and Ease: After the same manner as Wise Nature hath placed the Seeds in the Center of Apples, the Kernels in the middle of their Fruits; and in the same manner as the Onion, under the cover of so many Coats that encompass ·ves that precious Bud from ·llions of others are to have their being. For an Apple is in it self a little Universe; the Seed, hotter than the other parts thereof, is its Sun, which diffuses about it self that natural Heat which preserves its Globe: And in the Onion, the Germ is the little Sun of that little World, which vivifies and nourishes the vegetative Salt of that little mass. Having laid down this, then, for a ground, I say, That the Earth standing in need of the Light, Heat, and Influence of this great Fire, it turns round it, that it may receive in all parts alike that Virtue which keeps it in Being. For it would be as ridiculous to think, that that vast luminous Body turned about a point that it has not the least need of; as to imagine, that when we see a roasted Lark, that the Kitchin-fire must have turned round it. Else, were it the part of the Sun to do that drudgery, it would seem that the Physician stood in need of the Patient; that the Strong should yield to the Weak; the Superior serve the Inferior; and that the Ship did not sail about the Land, but the Land about the Ship.

"Now if you cannot easily conceive how so ponderous a Body can move; Pray, tell me, are the Stars and Heavens, which, in your Opinion, are so solid, any way lighter? Besides, it is not so difficult for us, who are assured of the Roundness of the Earth, to infer its motion from its Figure: But why do ye suppose the Heaven to be round, seeing you cannot know it, and that yet, if it hath not this Figure, it is impossible it can move? I object not to you your *Excentricks* nor *Epicycles*,[1] which you cannot explain but very confusedly, and which are out of doors in my Systeme.   Let's reflect only on the natural Causes of that Motion.   To make good your Hypothesis, you are forced to have recourse to Spirits or *Intelligences*, that move and govern your

⋯⋯ ⁻otion of the moon, for instance, was ex-
⋯ Ptolemaic system as an epicycle car-
⋯excentric; the centre of the excentric
⋯ the earth in a direction opposite to
⋯ epicycle.

Spheres. But for my part, without disturbing the repose of the supreme Being, who, without doubt, hath made Nature entirely perfect, and whose Wisdom ought so to have compleated her, that being perfect in one thing, she should not have been defective in another: I say, that the Beams and Influences of the Sun, darting Circularly upon the Earth, make it to turn as with a turn of the Hand we make a Globe to move; or, which is much the same, that the Steams which continually evaporate from that side of it which the Sun shines upon, being reverberated by the Cold of the middle Region, rebound upon it, and striking obliquely do of necessity make it whirle about in that manner.

"The Explication of the other Motions[1] is less perplexed still; for pray, consider a little—" At these words the Vice-Roy interrupted me: "I had

[1] The French has: "of the *two* other motions": *i.e.*, the movement of the fixed stars, and that of the planets.

rather," said he, "you would excuse your self from that trouble; for I have read some Books of *Gassendus*[1] on that subject: And hear what one of our Fathers, who maintained your Opinion one day, answered me. 'Really,' said he, 'I fancy that the Earth does move, not for the Reasons alledged by *Coper-*

[1] *Gassendus* or *Gassendi* was Cyrano's own teacher of Philosophy. Of Provençal origin, and at first Professor in the University of Aix, he came to Paris in 1641, and gave both private lessons and public courses as Professor of the Collège Royal. It was in one of his private classes that Cyrano was a fellow-student with Chapelle, Hesnaut, Bernier, and almost certainly Molière; the most important group of young "libertins" (*i.e.,* free-thinkers) of the epoch.

Gassendi was a bitter opponent of the supposedly Aristotelian school-philosophy of the time; and was on the whole the leader of those who in the seventeenth century followed Epicurean methods in thought. He is the author of a life of Epicurus, and an exposition of his philosophy. He was also an opponent of Descartes, being the most important contemporary supporter of empiricism as against the essentially idealistic method of Descartes.

He is important also as a popularizer of the Copernican system, by his Life of Copernicus, and his *Institutio Astronomica* (1647).

nicus ; but because Hell-fire being shut up in the Center of the Earth, the damned, who make a great bustle to avoid its Flames, scramble up to the Vault, as far as they can from them, and so make the Earth to turn, as a Turn-spit[1] makes the Wheel go round when he runs about in it.' "

We applauded that Thought, as being a pure effect of the Zeal of that good Father: And then the Vice-Roy told me, That he much wondered, how the Systeme of *Ptolemy*, being so improbable, should have been so universally received. "Sir," said I to him, "most part of Men, who judge of all things by the Senses, have suffered themselves to be perswaded by their Eyes; and as he who Sails along a Shoar thinks the Ship immoveable, and the Land in motion; even so Men turning with the Earth round the Sun have thought that it was the Sun that moved about them.

[1] A dog trained to turn a spit, by running about in a rotary cage attached to it. The French has simply: "as a *dog* makes a wheel turn, when he runs about in it."

To this may be added the unsupportable Pride of Mankind, who perswade themselves that Nature hath only been made for them; as if it were likely that the Sun, a vast Body Four hundred and thirty four times bigger than the Earth,[1] had only been kindled to ripen their Medlars and plumpen their Cabbage.

"For my part, I am so far from complying with their Insolence, that I believe the Planets are Worlds about the Sun, and that the fixed Stars are also Suns which have Planets about them, that's to say, Worlds, which because of their smallness, and that their borrowed light cannot reach us, are not discernable by Men in this World: For in good earnest, how can it be imagined that such spacious Globes are no more but vast Desarts; and that ours, because we live in it, hath been framed for the habitation of a dozen of proud Dandyprats?

[1] Cyrano had probably learned this from his master Gassendi. *Cf.* his "Epistola XX. de apparente magnitudine solis," 1641.   Modern Gas-
say the sun is 1,300,000 times greater than
h in volume, 316,000 times in mass.

How, must it be said, because the Sun measures our Days and Years, that it hath only been made to keep us from running our Heads against the Walls? No, no, if that visible Deity shine upon Man, it's by accident, as the King's Flamboy by accident lightens a Porter that walks along the Street:"

"But," said he to me, "[if,] as you affirm, the fixed Stars be so many Suns, it will follow that the World is infinite; seeing it is probable that the People of that World which moves about that fixed Star you take for a Sun, discover above themselves other fixed Stars, which we cannot perceive from hence, and so others in that manner *in infinitum*."

"Never question," replied I, "but as God could create the Soul Immortal, He could also make the World Infinite; if so it be, that Eternity is nothing else but an illimited Duration, and an *infinite*, a boundless Extension: And then God himself would be Finite, supposing the World not to be infinite; seeing he cannot be where nothing is, and that he could not encrease the greatness of the World without adding somewhat to his own Being, by beginning to exist where he did not exist before. We must believe then, that as from hence we see *Saturn* and *Jupiter ;* if we were in either of the Two, we should discover a great many Worlds which we perceive not; and that the Universe extends so *in infinitum.*"

"I' faith," replied he, "when you have said all you can, I cannot at all comprehend that Infinitude." "Good now," replied I to him, "do you comprehend the Nothing that is beyond it?   Not at all. For when you think of that *Nothing*, you imagine it at least to be like Wind or Air, and that is a Being: But if you conceive not an *Infinite* in general, you comprehend it at least in particulars; seeing it is not difficult to fancy to our selves, beyond the Earth, Air, and Fire which we see, other Air, and other Earth, and other Fire.   Now Infinitude is nothing else but a boundless Series of all these. But if you ask me, How these Worlds have been made, seeing Holy Scripture speaks only of one that God made? My answer is, That I have no more to say: For to oblige me to give a Reason for every thing that comes into my Imagination, is to stop my Mouth, and make me confess that in things of that nature my Reason shall always stoop to Faith."

He ingeniously [1] acknowledged to me that his Question was to be censured, but bid me pursue my notion: So that I went on, and told him, That all the other Worlds, which are not seen, or but imperfectly believed, are no more but the Scum that purges out of the Suns. For how could these great Fires subsist without some matter, that served them for Fewel? Now as the Fire drives from it the Ashes that would stifle it, or the Gold in a Crucible separates from the Marcasite [2] and Dross, and is refined

---

[1] *Ingenuously.* The two words were interchangeable in the seventeenth century.

[2] Iron pyrites.

3

to the highest Standard; nay, and as our Stomack discharges it self by vomit, of the Crudities that oppress it; even so these Suns daily evacuate, and reject the Remains of matter that might incommode their Fire: But when they have wholly consumed that matter which entertains[1] them; you are not to doubt, but they spread themselves abroad on all sides to seek for fresh Fewel, and fasten upon the Worlds which heretofore they have made, and particularly upon those that are nearest: Then these great Fires, reconcocting all the · Bodies, will as formerly force them out again, *Pell-mell*, from all parts; and being by little and little purified, they'll begin to serve for Suns to other little Worlds, which they procreate by driving them out of their Spheres: And that without doubt, made the *Pythagoreans* foretel the universal Conflagration.

---

[1] *Supports, feeds; cf.* Shakspere, *Richard III.*

" I'll be at charges for a looking-glass,
    And entertain a score or two of tailors."

"This is no ridiculous Imagination,
for *New-France* where we are, gives us
a very convincing instance of it. The
vast Continent of *America* is one half
of the Earth, which in spight of our
Predecessors, who a Thousand times
had cruised the Ocean, was not at that
time discovered: Nor, indeed, was it
then in being, no more than a great
many Islands, Peninsules, and Mountains that have since started up in our
Globe, when the Sun purged out its
Excrements to a convenient distance,
and of a sufficient Gravity to be attracted by the Center of our World;
either in small Particles, perhaps, or,
it may be also, altogether in one lump.
That is not so unreasonable but that *St.
Austin*[1] would have applauded to it, if
that Country had been discovered in his
Age. Seeing that great Man, who had
a very clear Wit, assures us, That in his
time the Earth was flat like the floor
of an Oven, and that it floated upon the
Water, like the half of an Orange: But

[1] St. Augustine.

if ever I have the honour to see you in *France*, I'll make you observe, by means of a most excellent Celescope, that some Obscurities, which from hence appear to be Spots, are Worlds a forming."

My Eyes that shut with this Discourse, obliged the Vice-Roy to withdraw.

CHAPTER IV.

Of how at last he set out again for the Moon, tho without his own Will.

Next Day, and the Days following, we had some Discourses to the
same purpose: But some time after,
since the hurry of Affairs suspended
our Philosophy, I fell afresh upon the
design of mounting up to the Moon.

So soon as she was up, I walked
about musing in the Woods, how I
might manage and succeed in my Enterprise; and at length on *St. John's-*[1]
Eve, when they were at Council in the
Fort, whether they should assist the
Wild Natives of the Country against the
Iroqueans; I went all alone to the top
of a little Hill at the back of our Habitation, where I put in Practice what you

[1] The Feast of St. John the Baptist, June 24.

shall hear.   I had made a Machine
which I fancied might carry me up as
high as I pleased, so that nothing seem-
ing to be wanting to it, I placed my
self within, and from the Top of a
Rock threw my self in the Air: But
because I had not taken my measures
aright, I fell with a sosh in the Valley
below.

Bruised as I was, however, I returned to my Chamber without loos-
ing courage, and with Beef-Marrow I
anointed my Body, for I was all over
mortified from Head to Foot: Then
having taken a dram of Cordial Waters
to strengthen my Heart, I went back to
look for my Machine; but I could not
find it, for some Soldiers, that had been
sent into the Forest to cut wood for a
Bonefire, meeting with it by chance,
had carried it with them to the Fort:
Where after a great deal of guessing
what it might be, when they had discovered the invention of the Spring,
some said, that a good many Fire-
Works should be fastened to it, because

CYRANO IN HIS STUDY.

—*From a 17th Century Engraving.*

their Force carrying them up on high, and the Machine playing its large Wings, no Body but would take it for a Fiery Dragon. In the mean time I was long in search of it, but found it at length in the Market-place of *Kebeck* (Quebec), just as they were setting Fire to it. I was so transported with Grief, to find the Work of my Hands in so great Peril, that I ran to the Souldier that was giving Fire to it, caught hold of his Arm, pluckt the Match out of his Hand, and in great rage threw my self into my Machine, that I might undo the Fire-Works that they had stuck about it; but I came too late, for hardly were both my Feet within, when whip, away went I up in a Cloud.

The Horror and Consternation I was in did not so confound the faculties of my Soul, but I have since remembered all that happened to me at that instant. For so soon as the Flame had devoured one tier of Squibs, which were ranked by six and six, by means of a Train that reached every half-dozen, another tier went off, and then another;[1] so that the Salt-Peter taking Fire, put off the danger by encreasing it. However, all the combustible matter being spent, there was a period put to the Fire-work; and whilst I thought of nothing less than to knock my Head against the top of some Mountain, I felt, without the least stirring, my elevation continuing; and adieu Machine, for I saw it fall down again towards the Earth.

That extraordinary Adventure puffed up my Heart with so uncommon a Gladness; that, ravished to see my self delivered from certain danger, I had the impudence to philosophize upon it. Whilst then with Eyes and Thought I cast about to find what might be the cause of it, I perceived my flesh blown

---

[1] *Cf.* the play of *Cyrano de Bergerac*, act III., scene xi.: "Or else, mechanic as well as artificer, I could have fashioned a giant grasshopper, with steel joints, which, impelled by successive explosions of saltpetre, would have hopped with me to the azure meadows where graze the starry flocks."

up, and still greasy with the Marrow, that I had daubed my self over with for the Bruises of my fall: I knew that the Moon being then in the Wain, and that it being usual for her in that Quarter to suck up the Marrow of Animals, she drank up that wherewith I was anointed, with so much the more force that her Globe was nearer to me, and that no interposition of Clouds weakened her Attraction.[1]

When I had, according to the computation I made since, advanced a good deal more than three quarters of the space that divided the Earth from the Moon; all of a sudden I fell with my Heels up and Head down, though I had made no Trip; and indeed, I had not been sensible of it, had not I felt my Head loaded under the weight of my Body: The truth is, I knew very well that I was not falling again tow-

[1] *Cf.*, in the play, the fifth of Cyrano's means for scaling the sky: "Since Phœbe, the moon-goddess, when she is at wane, is greedy, O beeves! of your marrow, . . . with that marrow have besmeared myself!"

ards our World; for though I found my self to be betwixt two Moons, and easily observed, that the nearer I drew to the one, the farther I removed from the other; yet I was certain, that ours was the bigger Globe of the two: Because after one or two days Journey, the remote Refractions of the Sun, confounding the diversity of Bodies and Climates, it appeared to me only as a large Plate of Gold: That made me imagine, that I byassed[1] towards the Moon; and I was confirmed in that Opinion, when I began to call to mind, that I did not fall till I was past three quarters of the way.   For, said I to my self, that Mass being less than ours, the Sphere of its Activity must be of less Extent also; and by consequence, it was later before I felt the force of its Center.

[1] The translator has apparently misread *biaisais* where the French editions have *baissais:* i.e., I *was descending* toward the moon.

CHAPTER V.

Of his Arrival there, and of the Beauty of that Country in which he fell.

In fine, after I had been a very long while in falling, as I judged, for the violence of my Precipitation hindered me from observing it more exactly: The last thing I can remember is, that I found my self under a Tree, entangled with three or four pretty large Branches which I had broken off by my fall; and my face besmeared with an Apple, that had dashed against it.

By good luck that place was, as you shall know by and by * * * * * *[1] So

[1] "That place was," unquestionably, the Garden of Eden, which Cyrano heretically locates in the Moon; and the "Tree" through which he has fallen, and an "Apple" of which has besmeared his face and recalled him to life, is the Tree of Life, that stood "in the midst of the garden."

This is the first of a series of hiatuses, which occur in all the French editions as well as the Eng-

that you may very well conclude, that
had it not been for that Chance, if I had

lish, and which are marked by those stars that
Cyrano refers to in the play: "But I intend setting all this down in a book, and the golden stars
I have brought back caught in my shaggy mantle,
when the book is printed, will be seen serving as
asterisks."

Lebret speaks of these gaps in his preface, saying he would have tried to fill them but for fear of
mixing his style with Cyrano's: "For the melancholy colour of my style will not let me imitate the
gayety of his; nor can my Wit follow the fine
flights of his Imagination."

It seems altogether improbable, however, that
Cyrano himself left the work thus incomplete, as
Lebret would imply. And in fact we can supply
from a Manuscript recently acquired (1890) by the
Bibliothèque Nationale, a long passage not printed
by Lebret (see pp. 60 ff.). There can be little doubt
that the passages were deliberately *cut out* by some
one on account of their "heretical" character. It
even seems probable, from passages at the beginning of the *Voyage to the Sun*, that when the work
was circulated in Manuscript, Cyrano had been the
object of persecution on account of them.

The passages lacking were cut out then—but by
whom? The usually accepted opinion is that of
our English translator, who says the gaps are
"occasioned, not by the Negligence of our Witty
French Author, but by the accursed Plagiary of
some rude Hand, that in his sickness rifted his
Trunks and stole his Papers, as he himself complains." M. Brun has suggested, however, and

had a thousand lives, they had been all lost.   I have many times since reflected upon the vulgar Opinion, That if one precipitate himself from a very high place, his breath is out before he reach the ground; and from my adventure I conclude it to be false, or else that the efficacious Juyce of that Fruit,[1] which squirted into my mouth, must needs have recalled my soul, that was not far from my Carcass, which was still hot and in a disposition of exerting the Functions of Life.   The truth is, so with some plausibility, that Lebret himself was responsible for the omissions; and that he thus continued, after Cyrano's death, his lifelong attempts at reforming and toning down the impolitic, unorthodox notions of his too-independent friend. So Cyrano was conquered once more in his battle with "les Compromis, les Préjugés, les Lâchetés," and finally "la Sottise":

" Je sais bien qu' à la fin vous me mettrez à bas;
   N'importe! je me bats, je me bats, je me bats!"

We are proud of printing for the first time in any edition of the *Voyage to the Moon*, at least a part of what had been cut out; and of being able to indicate for the first time what must have been the substance of the other lost passages, and what is the sense of the fragments preserved.

[1] The Apple of the Tree of Life.

soon as I was upon the ground my pain
was gone, before I could think what it
was; and the Hunger, which I felt during my Voyage, was fully satisfied with
the sense that I had lost it.[1]

When I was got up, I had hardly
taken notice of the largest of Four
great Rivers, which by their conflux
make a Lake; when the Spirit, or invisible Soul, of Plants that breath upon
that Country, refreshed my Brain with
a delightful smell: And I found that
the Stones there were neither hard nor
rough; but that they carefully softened
themselves when one trode upon them.

[2] I presently lighted upon a Walk with
five Avenues, in figure like to a Star;
the Trees whereof seemed to reach up

[1] The translation is not fully adequate here; the
French means: ". . . was fully satisfied, and left
me in its place only a slight memory of having
lost it."

[2] This beautiful Nature-description, the like of
which cannot be found in all seventeenth-century
French literature outside of Cyrano's works, was
apparently his favorite passage, since it is the only
one he has used twice. Cf. his Lettre XI., "D'une
maison de campagne."

to the Skie, a green plot of lofty Boughs:
Casting up my Eyes from the root to
the top, and then making the same Sur-
vey downwards, I was in doubt whether
the Earth carried them, or they the
Earth, hanging by their Roots: Their
high and stately Forehead seemed also
to bend, as it were by force, under the
weight of the Celestial Globes; and
one would say, that their Sighs and out-
stretched Arms, wherewith they em-
braced the Firmament, demanded of
the Stars the bounty of their purer Influences before they had lost any thing
of their Innocence in the contagious
Bed of the Elements. The Flowers
there on all hands, without the aid of
any other Gardiner but Nature, send
out so sweet (though wild) a Perfume,
that it rouzes and delights the Smell:
There the incarnate of a Rose upon the
Bush, and the lively Azure of a Violet
under the Rushes, captivating the
Choice, make each of themselves to be
judged the Fairest: There the whole
Year is Spring; there no poysonous

Plant sprouts forth, but is as soon destroyed; there the Brooks by an agreeable murmuring, relate their Travels to the Pebbles; there Thousands of Quiristers make the Woods resound with their melodious Notes; and the quavering Clubs of these divine Musicians are so universal, that every Leaf of the Forest seems to have borrowed the Tongue and shape of a Nightingale; nay, and the Nymph *Eccho* is so delightful[1] with their Airs, that to hear her repeat, one would say, She were sollicitous to learn them. On the sides of that Wood are Two Meadows, whose continued Verdure seems an Emerauld reaching out of sight.   The various Colours, which the Spring bestows upon the numerous little Flowers that grow there, so delightfully confounds and mingles their Shadows, that it is hard to be known, whether these Flowers shaken with a gentle Breeze pursue themselves, or fly rather from the Caresses of the Wanton *Zephyrus;* one

[1] In the literal sense, *full of delight*, delighted.

would likewise take that Meadow for an
Ocean, because, as the Sea, it presents
no Shoar to the view; insomuch, that
mine Eye fearing it might lose it self,
having roamed so long, and discovered
no Coast, sent my Thoughts presently
thither; and my Thoughts, imagining
it to be the end of the World, were
willing to be perswaded, that such
charming places had perhaps forced
the Heavens to descend and join the
Earth there.   In the midst of that vast
and pleasant Carpet, a rustick Fountain
bubbles up in Silver Purles, crowning
its enamelled Banks with Sets of Violets, and multitudes of other little
Flowers, that seem to strive which
shall first behold it self in that Chrystal
Myrroir: It is as yet in the Cradle, being but newly Born, and its Young and
smooth Face shews not the least Wrin-
kle.   The large Compasses it fetches,
in circling within it self, demonstrate
its unwillingness to leave its native
Soyl: And as if it had been ashamed to
be caressed in presence of its Mother,

4

with a Murmuring it thrust back my
hand that would have touched it: The
Beasts that came to drink there, more
rational than those of our World,
seemed surprised to see it day upon the
Horizon, whilst the Sun was with the
Antipodes; and durst not bend downwards upon the Brink, for fear of falling into the Firmament.

I must confess to you, That at the
sight of so many Fine things, I found
my self tickled with these agreeable
Twitches, which they say the *Embryo*
feels upon the infusion of its Soul: My
old Hair fell off, and gave place for
thicker and softer Locks: I perceived
my Youth revived, my face grow rud-
dy, my natural Heat mingle gently
again with my radical Moisture: And
in a word, I grew younger again by at
least Fourteen Years.

CHAPTER VI.

Of a Youth whom he met there, and of
their Conversation : what that country
was, and the Inhabitants of it.

I had advanced half a League,
through a Forest of Jessamines and
Myrtles, when I perceived something
that stirred, lying in the Shade: It was
a Youth, whose Majestick Beauty
forced me almost to Adoration. He
started up to hinder me; crying, "It is
not to me but to God that you owe
these Humilities." "You see one," answered I, "stunned with so many Wonders that I know not what to admire
most; for coming from a World, which
without doubt you take for a Moon
here, I thought I had arrived in another, which our Worldlings call a Moon
also; and behold I am in Paradice at
the Feet of a God, who will not be

Adored." "Except the quality¹ of a
God," replied he, "whose Creature I
only am, the rest you say is true: This
Land is the Moon, which you see from
your Globe, and this place where you
are is * * * * * * * * * *"²

"Now at that time Man's Imagination was so strong, as not being as yet
corrupted, neither by Debauches, the
Crudity of Aliments, nor the altera-
tions of Diseases, that being excited by
a violent desire of coming to this Sanc-
tuary, and his Body becoming light
through the heat of this Inspiration;
he was carried thither in the same man-

---

¹ "Quality" = *title*, as often in the seventeenth
century; *cf.* Shakspere, *Henry V.:*

   "Gentlemen of blood and quality."

² Probably a long passage has been lost here, in
which the "Youth" (the Prophet Elijah, who had
"translated" himself hither and become young by
eating of the Tree of Life) describes the place
where they are as the original Garden of Eden;
and tells of the Creation, the Fall, and the Ban-
ishment of Adam and Eve. At the beginning of
the next paragraph he is still speaking, and telling of Adam's transference from the Moon to the
Earth.

ner, as some Philosophers, who having fixed their Imagination upon the contemplation of a certain Object have sprung up in the Air by Ravishments, which you call Extasies. The Woman, who through the infirmity of her Sex was weaker and less hot, could not, without doubt, have the imagination strong enough to make the Intension of her Will prevail over the Ponderousness of her Matter; but because there were very few * * * * the Sympathy which still united that half to its whole,[1] drew her towards him as he mounted up, as the Amber attracts the Straw, [as] the Load-stone turns towards the North from whence it hath been taken, and drew to him that part of himself, as the Sea draws the Rivers which proceed from it. When they arrived in your Earth, they dwelt betwixt *Mesopotamia* and *Arabia*:[2] Some People knew them by the name

[1] The woman to the man, from whose side she was taken. Probably only a few words have been omitted at the last hiatus.

[2] The supposed situation of the Earthly Paradise.

of * * * *,[1] and others under that of *Prometheus*, whom the Poets feigned to have stolen Fire from Heaven, by reason of his Off-spring, who were endowed with a Soul as perfect as his own: So that to inhabit your World, that Man left this destitute; but the All-wise would not have so blessed an Habitation, to remain without Inhabitants; He suffered a few ages after that * * * * * * * * * * * * *[2] cloyed with the company of Men, whose Innocence was corrupted, had a desire to forsake them.   This person,[3] however, thought no retreat secure enough from the Ambition of Men, who already Murdered one another about the distribution of your World; except that blessed Land, which his Grand-Father[4]

---

[1] Adam and Eve.

[2] We may imagine this a short hiatus, to be filled in as follows: "He suffered a few ages after that, *that a holy man, whose name was Enoch*, cloyed with the company of men. . . . " etc.

[3] Enoch. On his translation, which Cyrano here makes Elijah account for, see Genesis, chapter v.

[4] Adam. Cyrano may possibly have confused

had so often mentioned unto him, and
to which no Body had as yet found
out the way: But his Imagination
supplied that; for seeing he had observed that * * * he filled Two large
Vessels which he sealed Hermetically,
and fastened them under his Arm-pits:
So soon as the Smoak began to rise upwards, and could not pierce through the
Mettal, it forced up the Vessels on high,
and with them also that Great Man.[1]
When he was got as high as the Moon,
and had cast his Eyes upon that lovely
Garden, a fit of almost supernatural Joy
convinced him, that that was the place
where his Grand-father had heretofore
lived. He quickly untied the Vessels,
which he had girt like Wings about his
Shoulders, and did it so luckily, that he
was scarcely Four Fathom in the Air

the Enoch who was translated with another Enoch
who was the son of Cain and so grandson of Adam.
But it is more probable that he used the word
aïeul in its common sense of *ancestor;* as indeed
"grandfather" was used in old English.

[1] *Cf.* the play: "Since smoke by its nature as-
cends, I could have blown into an appropriate
globe a sufficient quantity to ascend with me."

above the Moon, when he set his Fins a going;[1] yet he was high enough still to have been hurt by the fall, had it not been for the large skirts of his Gown, which being swelled by the Wind, gently upheld him till he set Foot on ground.[2]   As for the two Vessels, they mounted up to a certain place, where they have continued: And those are they, which now a-days you call the *Balance*.

"I must now tell you, the manner how I came hither: I believe you have not forgot my name,[3] seeing it is not long since I told it you.   You shall know then, that I lived on the agreeable Banks of one of the most renowned Rivers of your World, where amongst my Books, I lead a Life pleasant enough not to be lamented, though it slipt away fast enough.   In the mean while, the more I increased in Knowl-

---

[1] " Qu'il prit congé de ses nageoires," = " when he *abandoned* his *floats* (or *bladders*)."

[2] Cyrano may here be credited with anticipating the idea of the parachute.

[3] Elijah.   The passage referred to is lost.

edge, the more I knew my Ignorance.
Our Learned Men never put me in
mind of the famous *Mada*,[1] but the
thoughts of his perfect Philosophy
made me to Sigh.   I was despairing of
being able to attain to it, when one day,
after a long and profound Studying. I
took a piece of Load-stone about two
Foot square, which I put into a Fur-
nace; and then after it was well purged,
precipitated and dissolved, I drew the
calcined Attractive of it, and reduced it
into the size of about an ordinary Bowl.[2]

"After the Preparations, I got a very
light Machine of Iron made, into which
I went, and when I was well seated
in my place, I threw this Magnetick
Bowl as high as I could up into the
Air.   Now the Iron Machine, which I
had purposely made more massive in
the middle than at the ends, was presently elevated, and in a just Poise; because the middle received the greatest
force of Attraction.   So then, as I ar-

---

[1] Spell the name backward.
[2] *Ball.* Cf. *Bowling.* Cf. also p. 177.

rived at the place whither my Load-
stone had attracted me, I presently
threw up my Bowl in the Air over me."[1]
"But," said I, interrupting him, "How
came you to heave up your Bowl so
streight over your Chariot, that it
never happened to be on one side of it?"
"That seems to me to be no wonder at
all," said he; "for the Load-stone being
once thrown up in the Air, drew the
Iron streight towards it; and so it was
impossible, that ever I should mount
side-ways. Nay more, I can tell you,
that when I held the Bowl in my hand,
I was still mounting upwards; because
the Chariot flew always to the Load-
stone, which I held over it. But the
effort of the Iron to be united to my
Bowl, was so violent that it made my
Body bend double; so that I durst but

[1] *Cf.* the "sixth means" in the play: "Or else, I
could have placed myself upon an iron plate, have
taken a magnet of suitable size, and thrown it in
the air! That way is a very good one! The magnet flies upward, the iron instantly after; the
'ooner overtaken than you fling it up
'he rest is clear! You can go upward

once essay that new Experiment. · The truth is, it was a very surprizing Spectacle to behold; for the Steel of that flying House, which I had very carefully Polished, reflected on all sides the light of the Sun with so great life and lustre, that I thought my self to be all on fire.[1] In fine, after often Bowling and following of my Cast, I came, as you did, to an Elevation from which I descended towards this World; and because at that instant I held my Bowl very fast between my hands, my Machine, whereof the Seat pressed me hard, that it might approach its Attractive, did not forsake me; all that now I feared was, that I should break my Neck: But to save me from that, ever now and then I tossed up my Bowl; that by its attractive Virtue it might prevent the violent Descent of my Machine, and render my fall more easie, as indeed it happened; for when I saw my self within Two or three hundred fathom of

---

[1] The "chariot of fire" in which Elijah was taken up into heaven. *Cf.* 2 Kings, ii. 11.

the Earth, I threw out my Bowl on all hands, level with the Chariot, sometimes on this side, and sometimes on that, until I came to a certain Distance; and immediately then, I tossed it up above me; so that my Machine following it, I left it, and let my self fall on the other side, as gently as I could, upon the Sand; insomuch that my fall was no greater than if it had been but my own height.   I shall not describe to you the amazement I was in at the sight of the wonders of this place, seeing it was so like the same, wherewith I just now saw you seized.   [¹ You shall know then, that on the morrow I met with the Tree of Life, by the means of which I have kept my self from growing old; it straightway consumed the Serpent ² and made him to vanish away in smoke."

¹ The following pages are translated from the text as printed for the first time, from the Manuscript at the *Bibliothèque Nationale*, in an appendix to M. Brun's thesis on Cyrano Bergerac, 1893.

² "The serpent," as soon appears, is *original sin*, which

　　ught *death* into the world, and all our woe."

At these words: "Venerable and holy patriarch," said I to him, "I am eager to know what you understand by that Serpent which was consumed." He, with face a smiling, answered me thus: . . .[1]

"The Tree of Knowledge is planted opposite; its fruit is covered with a Rind which produces Ignorance in whomsoever hath tasted thereof; yet this Rind preserves underneath its thickness all the spiritual virtues of this learned food. God, when he had driven Adam from this fortunate country, rubbed his gums with this same Rind, that he might never find the way back again; for more than fifteen years thereafter he did dote, and did so completely forget all things, that neither he nor any of his descendants till Moses ever remembered even so much as the Creation; but what Power was left of this direful Rind at last passed away through the warmth and

---

[1] Our author's treatment of "original sin" is, according to M. Brun, unprintable.

brightness of that great Prophet's genius.

" I happily met with one among these
apples, which through ripeness was
despoiled of its skin; hardly had my
mouth watered with it, when Universal
Knowledge penetrated my being, I felt
as it were an infinite number of Eyes
fix themselves in my head, and I knew
the means of speaking with the Lord.

" When I have since reflected on
these miraculous events, I have judged
that I could in no wise have overcome,
by any occult powers of a simple natural body, the vigilance of that Seraph
whom God has ordained to guard this
Paradise; but since he is pleased to use
second causes, I imagined that he had inspired me to find this means of entering
there; even as he thought good to take
of the ribs of Adam to make him a
wife, though he could form her of
Earth, as well as he did Adam.

" I remained long in this Garden,
walking about alone; but in fine, since
the angel that was Keeper of the Gate

seemed to me to be in chief my Host
here, I was taken with the desire to
salute him. In an hour's journey I
came to a place where a thousand
Lightnings mingled together in one
blinding light that served but to make
Darkness visible. I was not yet fully
recovered from this dazzlement, when I
saw before me a beautiful Young man.
'I am,' said he, 'the Archangel whom
you seek, I have but now read in God
that he had inspired you with the
means of coming here, and that he
willed you should here expect his pleasure.' He talked with me of many
things, and told me among the rest:
" That the light wherewith I had been
amazed was nothing fearful, but that it
appeared almost every evening when
he went his rounds, seeing that to avoid
sudden attack from the Evil Spirits,
which may enter secretly at any place,
he was constrained mightily to swing
his Flaming Sword in circles, all about
the bounds of the Earthly Paradise;
and that the light I had seen was the

lightnings which the steel of it gave forth. ' Those also which you perceive from your Earth,' he added, ' are of my creation. And if sometimes you see them at a great distance, it is because the clouds of some distant region hold themselves in such disposition as to receive an impression of these unbodied fires, and reflect them to your eyes; just as clouds otherwise disposed may prove themselves fit to make the Rain-bow.'

"I will not instruct you further in these matters, since to be sure the Apple of Knowledge is not far from hence; whereof as soon as you have eaten, you will know all things even as I. But see you make no mistake, for most of the Fruits that hang from that Plant are encased in a Rind, whose taste will abase you even below man; while the part within will make you mount up to be even as the Angels."

Elijah had come to this point of the teachings of the Seraph, when a little man came up with us; "This is

that Enoch of whom I told you," said
my guide to me apart; and even while
he finished the words, Enoch offered us
a basketful of I know not what fruits,
like to Pomegranates, which he had
but discovered that same day in a distant coppice. I took some and put in
my pockets, as Elijah bade me. Here-
upon Enoch asked him who I might be.
" That is a matter," answered my guide,
" to entertain us at more leisure; this
evening when we have withdrawn he
shall tell us himself of the miraculous
particulars of his journey."

With these words we arrived beneath
a sort of Hermitage, made of palm-
branches skilfully inter-laced with
myrtle and orange-branches. There
I saw, in a little nook, great piles of a
kind of floss-silk, so white and so delicate that one might take it for the vir-
gin Soul of the snow; and I saw dis-
taffs lying here and there; whereupon
I asked my guide what use they served.
" To spin," he answered me; " when
the good Enoch would relax his mind

from meditation, he applies himself sometimes to dressing this Lady-distaff, sometimes to weaving the cloth from which they make Shifts for the eleven thousand Virgins. Surely in your world you have met with that something white, which flutters on the winds in Autumn about the season of the Winter-sowings. Your peasant-folk call it Our Lady's Cotton, but it is no other than the Flock that Enoch purges his Linen of, when he cards it."

We made little delay there, and but barely took leave of Enoch, whom this cabin served for his Cell; in truth what made us leave him so soon was this: that he said some prayer there every six hours; and it was at least that time since he had finished the last one.

As we went forward, I begged Elijah to finish that history which he had begun, of the *Assumptions* or *Translations;* and I said, that he had come, I thought, to that of Saint *John* the Evangelist.

Then said he to me: "Since you have not the patience, to wait till the Apple of Knowledge teach you all these things better than I can, I will even tell you.   Know then that God——"

At this word, in some way I know not how, the Devil would have his Finger in that pie; or howsoever it came about, so it was that I could not forbear Interrupting him with raillery.

"I remember that case," said I: "God heard one day that the Soul of the Evangelist was so loosed from his Body, that he no more kept it in but by shutting his teeth hard; and at that moment the hour when he had foreseen that he should be translated hither was almost past; so having no time to get him a machine made ready for coming, He was constrained to make him suddenly *be* here, without having time to *bring* him."

During all my discourse Elijah bent upon me such a look, as would have been fit to kill me, had 1 then been capable of dying from aught but Hunger. "Thou Wretch," said he, and drew back in horror, "thou hast the insolence to rail at Holy Things! Surely thou shouldst not go unpunished, were it not that the All-wise determines to spare thee as a marvellous example of His long-suffering, a witness to the Nations. Get hence, thou Blasphemer, go thou and publish in this little World, and in the other (for thou art predestined to return thither), the unforgetting Hatred that God bears to Atheists."

Hardly had he finished this Curse, when he seized me roughly to drag me toward the Gate. When we were arrived beside a great Tree whose branches bent almost to Earth with the burden of their Fruit, "Here," said he, "is that Tree of Knowledge where thou shouldst have got Enlightenment inconceivable, but for thy Infidelity."

At that word I feigned to swoon with weakness, and letting my self fall against a low branch I handily filched an Apple from it. And in but a few strides more I was set down outside of that delicious Garden.

In that moment, being so violently pressed by Hunger, that I even forgot I was in the grip of the angry Prophet, I drew from my pocket one of those Apples I had filled it with, wherein I buried my teeth as deep as I could. But so it was, that in place of taking one of those Enoch had given me, my hand fell on that very Apple I had plucked from the Tree of Knowledge, which for my misfortune I had not freed of its Rind.]

[1] Scarcely had I tasted it, when a thick Cloud over-cast my Soul: I saw no body now near me; and in the whole Hemisphere my Eyes could not discern the least Tract of the way I had made; yet nevertheless I fully remembered every thing that befel me. When I reflected since upon that Miracle, I fanced that the skin of the Fruit which I bit had not rendered me altogether brutish;

[1] Here the original text resumes, as found in all the editions, both French and English.

because my Teeth piercing through it were a little moistened by the Juyce within, the efficacy whereof had dissipated the Malignities of the Rind. I was not a little surprised to see my self all alone, in a Country I knew not. It was to no purpose for me to stare and look about me; for no Creature appeared to comfort me.

CHAPTER VII.

Being cast out from that Country, of the
new Adventures *which Befell him ;*
and of the Demon *of* Socrates.

At length I resolved to march forwards, till Fortune should aford me the
company of some Beasts, or at least
the means of Dying. She favourably
granted my desire; for within half a
quarter of a League, I met two huge
Animals, one of which stopt before me,
and the other fled swiftly to its Den;
for so I thought at least; because that
some time after, I perceived it come
back again in company of above Seven
or Eight hundred of the same kind, who
beset me. When I could discern them
at a near distance, I perceived that they
were proportioned and shaped like us.
This adventure brought into my mind
the old Wives Tales of my Nurse con-

cerning *Syrenes*, *Faunes* and *Satyrs*:
Ever now and then they raised such
furious Shouts, occasioned undoubtedly
by their Admiration ' at the sight of
me, that I thought I was e'en turned
a Monster.   At length one of these
Beast-like men, catching hold of me by
the Neck, just as Wolves do when they
carry away Sheep, tossed me upon his
back and brought me into their Town:
where I was more amazed than before,
when I knew they were Men, that I
could meet with none of them but who
marched upon all four.

When these People saw that I was so
little, (for most of them are Twelve
Cubits long,) and that I walked only
upon Two Legs, they could not believe
me to be a Man: For they were of
opinion, that Nature having given to
men as well as Beasts Two Legs and
Two Arms, they should both make use
of them alike.   And, indeed, reflecting
upon that since, that scituation of Body
did not seem to me altogether extrava-

---

¹ Astonishment.

gant; when I called to mind, that whilst Children are still under the nurture of Nature, they go upon all four, and that they rise not on their two Legs but by the care of their Nurses; who set them in little running Chairs, and fasten straps to them, to hinder them from falling on all four, as the only posture that the shape of our Body naturally inclines to rest in.

They said then, (as I had it interpreted to me since) That I was infallibly the Female of the Queens little Animal. And therefore as such, or somewhat else, I was carried streight to the Town-House, where I observed by the muttering and gestures both of the People and Magistrates, that they were consulting what sort of a thing I could be. When they had conferred together a long while, a certain Burgher, who had the keeping of the strange Beasts, besought the Mayor and Aldermen to commit me to his Custody, till the Queen should send for me to couple me to my Male. This was granted without any difficulty, and that Juggler carried me to his House; where he taught me to Tumble, Vault, make Mouths, and shew a Hundred odd Tricks, for which in the Afternoons he received Money at the door from those that came in to see me.

But Heaven pitying my Sorrows, and vext to see the Temple of its Maker profaned, so ordered it, that one day [when] I was tied to a Rope, wherewith the Mountebank made me Leap and Skip to divert the People, I heard a Man's voice, who asked me what I was, in Greek.   I was much surprised to hear one speak in that Country as they do in our World.   He put some Questions to me, which I answered, and then gave him a full account of my whole design, and the success of my Travels: He took the pains to comfort me, and, as I take it, said to me: "Well, Son, at length you suffer for the frailties of your World: There is a Mobile ' here, as well as there, that can

¹ Mobile = people, populace.   *Cf.* p. 145.

sway with nothing but what they are accustomed to: But know, that you are but justly served; for had any one of this Earth had the boldness to mount up to yours, and call himself a Man, your Sages would have destroyed him as a Monster."

He then told me, That he would acquaint the Court with my disaster; adding, that so soon as he had heard the news that went of me, he came to see me, and was satisfied that I was a man of the World of which I said I was; because he had Travelled there formerly, and sojourned in *Greece*, where he was called the *Demon of Socrates:* That after the Death of that Philosopher, he had governed and taught *Epaminondas* at *Thebes:* After which being gone over to the *Romans*, Justice had obliged him to espouse the party of the Younger *Cato:* That after his Death, he had addicted himself to *Brutus:* That all these great Men having left in that World no more but the shadow of their Virtues, he with his

Companions had retreated to Temples and Solitudes. "In a word," added he, "the People of your World became so dull and stupid, that my Companions and I lost all the Pleasure that formerly we had had in instructing them: Not but that you have heard Men talk of us; for they called us *Oracles, Nymphs, Geniuses, Fairies, Houshold-Gods, Lemmes,*[1] *Larves,*[2] *Lamiers,*[3] *Hobgoblins, Nayades, Incubusses, Shades, Manes, Visions* and *Apparitions:* We abandoned your World, in the Reign of *Augustus,* not long after I had appeared to *Drusus* the Son of *Livia,* who waged War in *Germany,* whom I forbid to proceed any farther. It is not long since I came from thence a second time; within these Hundred Years I had a Commission to Travel thither: I roamed a great deal in *Europe,* and conversed with

[1] Lemures; malicious spirits of the dead. *Cf.* Milton:

"The Lars and Lemures moan with midnight plaint."

[2] Lars, larvas; ghosts, spectres.

[3] Lamias; female demons or vampires.

some, whom possibly you may have known. One Day, amongst others, I appeared to *Cardan*,[1] as he was at his Study; I taught him a great many things, and he in acknowledgment promised me to inform Posterity of whom he had those Wonders, which he intended to leave in writing.[2] There I saw *Agrippa*,[3] the Abbot *Trithemius*,[4] Doctor *Faustus*, *La Brosse*, *Cæsar*,[5] and a certain Cabal of Young Men, who are commonly called *Rosacrucians*[6] or

[1] *Cf.* p. 12, n. 1.

[2] "Jerome Cardan pretended to have written most of his books under the dictation of a Familiar Spirit . . . but, in his treatise *De Rerum Varietate*, he ingenuously declares that he had never had any other genius but his own : *Ego certe nullum dæmonem aut genium mihi adesse cognosco.*" (Note of Paul Lacroix.)

[3] Cornelius Agrippa of Nettesheim, 1486–1535, philosopher, astrologer, and alchemist. Cyrano introduces him in his *Lettre XII.*, "Pour les Sorciers."

[4] Jean Trithème (or Johann Tritheim), Abbot of Spanheim; a man of universal scholarship, and an experimenter in alchemy; also accused of sorcery.

[5] César de Nostradamus, physician and astrologer of the early sixteenth century.

[6] A famous occult order which probably never

Knights of the Red-Cross, whom I taught a great many Knacks and Secrets of Nature, which without doubt have made them pass for great Magicians: I knew *Campanella*[1] also; it was I that advised him, whilst he was in the Inquisition at *Rome*, to put his Face and Body into the usual Postures of those whose inside he needed to know, that by the same frame of Body he might excite in himself the thoughts which the same scituation had raised in his Adversaries; because by so doing, he might better manage their Soul, when he came

existed, but about which much was written in the first half of the seventeenth century. It was supposed to have been founded early in the fifteenth century by Rosenkrenz, a pilgrim who had acquired all the wisdom of the Orient.

[1] Tomaso Campanella, 1568–1639, Italian poet and philosopher, who came to Paris in 1634. His philosophy was much admired by Cyrano, since he rejected the Aristotelism of the schools, advocated empiricism as the only method of arriving at truth, and insisted on the "four Elements" as the origin of all things.

He appears as an important character in Cyrano's *Voyage to the Sun*, where he is Cyrano's companion and guide to the Land of the Philosophers.

to know it; and at my desire he began a Book, which we Entituled, *De Sensu Rerum.*[1]

"I likewise haunted, in *France*, *La Mothe le Vayer*[2] and *Gassendus*;[3] this last hath written as much like a Philosopher, as the other lived: I have known a great many more there, whom your Age call *Divines*,[4] but all that I could find in them was a great deal of Babble and a great deal of Pride. In fine, since I past over from your Country into *England*, to acquaint my self with the manners of its Inhabitants, I

---

[1] Campanella's principal work, published in 1620.

[2] François de La Mothe le Vayer, 1588–1672. He was the tutor of the Duc d'Orléans, brother of Louis XIV., and, after 1654, of Louis XIV. himself. In philosophy he was a free-thinker, in literature a disciple of Montaigne. He nevertheless concealed his scepticism in philosophy, even in his chief work, the *Doutes sceptiques*, under a pretended orthodoxy in religion, and so was never persecuted. Possibly it is to this that Cyrano refers in saying, that he " *lived* as much like a philosopher, as Gassendi wrote."

[3] *Cf.* p 28, n. 1.

[4] *Divine.* The translator has mistaken an adjective for a noun.

met with a Man, the shame of his Country; for certainly it is a great shame
for the Grandees of your States to
know the virtue which in him has its
Throne, and not to adore him: That I
may give you an Abridgement of his
Panegyrick, he is all Wit, all Heart, and
possesses all the Qualities, of which
one alone was heretofore sufficient to
make an Heroe: It was *Tristan* the
Hermite.[1] The Truth is, I must tell
you, when I perceived so exalted a Virtue I mistrusted it would not be taken
notice of, and therefore I endeavoured
to make him accept Three Vials, the
first filled with the Oyl of Talk,[2] the
other with the Powder of Projection,[3]

[1] François Tristan l'Hermite, 1601–1655, a French
dramatist of importance.   His tragedy of *Ma-
riamne*, in date contemporary with Corneille's *Cid*,
marks him as a predecessor of Racine in method
and manner. He is also the author of fugitive
verse, but neither that nor his plays make him
quite worthy of Cyrano's exalted "Elogy."

He was compelled to pass the years 1614–1620 in
England, on account of a duel fought at the age of
thirteen!   [2] Talc, silicate of magnesia.

[3] The "Philosopher's Stone," in form of powder,

and the third with *Aurum Potabile;*[1] but he refused them with a more generous Disdain than *Diogenes* did the Complements of *Alexander*. In fine, I can add nothing to the Elogy[2] of that Great Man, but that he is the only Poet, the only Philosopher, and the only Free-man amongst you: These are the considerable Persons that I conversed with; all the rest, at least that I know, are so far below Man that I have seen Beasts somewhat above them.

"After all, I am not a Native neither of this Country nor yours, I was born in the Sun; but because sometimes our World is overstock'd with people, by reason of the long Lives of the Inhabitants, and that there is hardly any Wars or Diseases amongst them: Our Magistrates, from time to time, send

for chemical "projection" upon baser metals, to transmute them into gold.

[1] The "Elixir of Life," or the "Philosopher's Stone" in liquid form.

[2] Eulogy. Still so used at the end of the eighteenth century.

6

Colonies into the neighbouring Worlds.
For my own part, I was commanded to
go to yours; being declared Chief of
the Colony that accompanyed me. I
came since into this World, for the
Reasons I told you; and that which
makes me continue here, is, because the
Men are great lovers of Truth; and have
no Pedants among them; that the Philosophers are never perswaded but by
Reason, and that the Authority of a
Doctor, or of a great number, is not
preferred before the Opinion of a
Thresher in a Barn, when he has right
on his side. In short, none are reckoned Mad-men in this Country, but
Sophisters and Orators." I asked him
how they lived? he made answer, three
or four thousand Years; and thus went
on:

"Though the Inhabitants of the Sun
be not so numerous as those of this
World; yet the Sun is many times over
stocked, because the People being of a
hot constitution are stirring and ambi-
tious, and digest much."

"You ought not to be surprised at what I tell you; for though our Globe be very vast, and yours little, though we die not before the end of Four thousand Years, and you at the end of Fifty; yet know, that as there are not so many Stones as clods of Earth, nor so many Animals as Plants, nor so many Men as Beasts; just so there ought not to be so many Spirits as Men, by reason of the difficulties that occur in the Generation of a perfect Creature."

I asked him, if they were Bodies as we are? He made answer, That they were Bodies, but not like us, nor any thing else which we judged such; because we call nothing a Body commonly, but what we can touch: That, in short, there was nothing in Nature but what was material; and that though they themselves were so, yet they were forced, when they had a mind to appear to us, to take Bodies proportionated to what our Senses are able to know; and that, without doubt, that was the rea-

son why many have taken the Stories
that are told of them for the Delusions
of a weak Fancy, because they only
appeared in the night time: He told
me withal, That seeing they were ne-
cessitated to piece together the Bodies
they were to make use of, in great
haste, many times they had not leisure
enough to render them the Objects of
more Senses than one at a time, sometimes of the Hearing, as the Voices of
Oracles, sometimes of the Sight, as the
Fires and *Visions*, sometimes of the
Feeling, as the *Incubusses;* and that
these Bodies being but Air condensed
in such or such a manner, the Light
dispersed them by its heat, in the same
manner as it scatters a Mist.

So many fine things as he told me,
gave me the curiosity to question him
about his Birth and Death; if in the
Country of the Sun, the *individual* was
procreated by the ways of Generation,
and if it died by the dissolution of its
Constitution, or the discomposure of its
Organs? "Your senses," replied he,

"bear but too little proportion to the Explication of these Mysteries: Ye Gentlemen imagine, that whatsoever you cannot comprehend is spiritual, or that it is
not at all; but that Consequence [1] is ab-
surd, and it is an argument, that there
are a Million of things, perhaps, in the
Universe, that would require a Million
of different Organs in you to understand them. For instance, I by my
Senses know the cause of the Sympathy that is betwixt the Load-stone and
the Pole, of the ebbing and flowing of
the Sea, and what becomes of the Animal after Death; you cannot reach
these high Conceptions but by Faith,
because they are Secrets above the
power of your Intellects; no more than
a Blind-man can judge of the beauties
of a Land-skip, the Colours of a Picture, or the streaks of a Rain-bow; or

---

[1] Consequence = *conclusion*, deduction. *Cf.* Mat-
thew Prior:

> " Can syllogisms set things right?
> No, majors soon with minors fight.
> Or both in friendly consort joined
> The consequence limps false behind."

at best he will fancy them to be somewhat palpable, to be like Eating, a Sound, or a pleasant Smell: Even so, should I attempt to explain to you what I perceive by the Senses which you want, you would represent it to your self as somewhat that may be Heard, Seen, Felt, Smelt or Tasted, and yet it is no such thing."

He was gone on so far in his Discourse, when my Juggler perceived, that the Company began to be weary of my Gibberish, that they understood not, and which they took to be an inarticulated Grunting: He therefore fell to pulling my Rope afresh to make me leap and skip, till the Spectators having had their Belly-fulls of Laughing, affirmed that I had almost as much Wit as the Beasts of their Country, and so broke up.

CHAPTER VIII.

Of the Languages *of the People in the Moon; of the Manner of Feeding there, and of* Paying *the Scot; and of how the Author was taken to Court.*

Thus, all the comfort I had during the misery of my hard Usage, were the visits of this officious[1] Spirit; for you may judge what conversation I could have with these that came to see me, since besides that they only took me for an Animal, in the highest class of the *Category* of Bruits, I neither understood their Language, nor they mine. For you must know, that there are but two Idioms in use in that Country, one for the Grandees, and another for the People in general.

[1] Officious = kindly, ready to serve, doing good offices. *Cf.* Milton, *Paradise Lost:*

" Yet, not to earth are those bright luminaries
 Officious; but to thee, earth's habitant."

That of the great ones is no more
but various inarticulate Tones, much
like to our Musick when the Words are
not added to the Air:[1] and in reality it
is an Invention both very useful and
pleasant; for when they are weary of
talking, or disdain to prostitute their
Throats to that Office, they take either
a Lute or some other Instrument,
whereby they communicate their
Thoughts as well as by their Tongue:
So that sometimes Fifteen or Twenty
in a Company will handle a point of
Divinity, or discuss the difficulties of a
Law-suit, in the most harmonious Con-
sort that ever tickled the Ear.

The second, which is used by the
Vulgar, is performed by a shivering of
the Members, but not, perhaps, as you

---

[1] *Cf. The Man in the Moone*, of Francis Godwin:
"Their Language is very difficult, since it hath no
Affinity with any other I ever heard, and consists
not so much of Words and Letters, as Tunes and
strange Sounds which no Letters can express; for
there are few Words but signify several Things,
and are distinguished only by their Sounds, which
are sung as it were in uttering; yea many Words
consist of Tunes only, without Words."

may imagine; for some parts of the
Body signifie an entire Discourse; for
example, the agitation of a Finger, a
Hand, an Ear, a Lip, an Arm, an Eye,
a Cheek, every one severally will make
up an Oration, or a Period with all the
parts of it: Others serve only instead
of Words, as the knitting of the Brows,
the several quiverings of the Muscles,
the turning of the Hands, the stamping
of the Feet, the contorsion of the Arm;
so that when they speak, as their Custom is, stark naked, their Members being used to gesticulate their Conceptions, move so quick that one would
not think it to be a Man that spoke, but
a Body that trembled.

Every day almost the Spirit came to
see me, and his rare Conversation made
me patiently bear with the rigour of
my Captivity. At length one morning
I saw a Man enter my Cabbin, whom I
knew not, who having a long while
licked me gently, took me in his Teeth
by the Shoulder, and with one of his
Paws, wherewith he held me up for

fear I might hurt my self, threw me
upon his Back; where I found my self
so softly seated, and so much at my
ease, that, [though] being afflicted to
be used like a Beast, I had not the least
desire of making my escape; and besides, these Men that go upon all four
are much swifter than we, seeing the
heaviest of them make nothing of running down a Stagg.

In the mean time I was extreamly
troubled that I had no news of my
courteous Spirit; and the first night
we came to our Inn, as I was walking in
the Court, expecting till Supper should
be ready, a pretty handsome young
Man came smiling in my Face and
cast his Two Fore-Legs about my Neck.
After I had a little considered him:
"How!" said he in *French*, "do you
[not] know your Friend then?" I leave
you to judge in what case I was at that
time; really, my surprise was so great,
that I began to imagine, that all the
Globe of the Moon, all that had befallen
me, and all that I had seen, had only

been Enchantment: And that Beast-man, who was the same that had car-ried me all day, continued to speak to me in this manner; "You promised me, that the good Offices I did you should never be forgotten, and yet it seems you have never seen me before;" but perceiving me still in amaze: "In fine," said he, "I am that same *Demon* of *Socrates*, who diverted you during your Imprisonment, and who, that I may still oblige you, took to my self a Body, on which I carried you to day:" "But," said I interrupting him, "how can that be, seeing that all Day you were of a very long Stature, and now you are very short; that all day long you had a weak and broken Voice, and now you have a clear and vigorous one; that, in short, all day long you were a Grey-headed old Man, and are now a brisk young Blade: Is it then that whereas in my Country, the Progress is from Life to Death; Animals here go Retro-grade from Death to Life, and by grow-ing old become young again."

"So soon as I had spoken to the Prince," said he, "and received orders to bring you to Court, I went and found you out where you were, and have brought you hither; but the Body I acted in was so tired out with the Journey, that all its Organs refused me their ordinary Functions, so that I enquired the way to the Hospital; where being come in I found the Body of a young Man, just then expired by a very odd Accident, but yet very common in this Country. I drew near him, pretending to find motion in him still, and protesting to those who were present, that he was not dead, and that what they thought to be the cause of his Death, was no more but a bare Lethargy; so that without being perceived, I put my Mouth to his, by which I entred as with a breath: Then down dropt my old Carcass, and as if I had been that young Man, I rose and came to look for you, leaving the Spectators crying a Miracle."

With this they came to call us to Sup-

per, and I followed my Guide into a
Parlour richly furnished; but where I
found nothing fit to be eaten.   No Victuals appearing, when I was ready to die
of Hunger, made me ask him where the
Cloath was laid: But I could not hear
what he answered, for at that instant
Three or Four young Boys, Children of
the House, drew near, and with much
Civility stript me to the Shirt.   This
new Ceremony so astonished me, that I
durst not so much as ask my Pretty
Valets de Chamber the cause of it; and
I cannot tell how my Guide, who asked
me what I would begin with, could
draw from me these two Words, *A
Potage;* but hardly had I pronounced
them, when I smelt the odour of the
most agreeable Soop that ever steamed
in the rich Gluttons Nose: I was about
to rise from my place, that I might
trace that delicious Scent to its source,
but my Carrier hindered me: " Whither
are you going," said he, " we shall fetch
a walk by and by; but now it is time to
Eat, make an end of your *Potage*, and

then we'll have something else:" "And
where the Devil is the *Potage?*" answered I half angry: "Have you laid a
wager you'll jeer me all this Day?" "I
thought," replied he, "that at the Town
we came from, you had seen your Master
or some Bo[dy] else at meal, and that's
the reason I told you not, how People
feed in this Country. Seeing then you
are still ignorant, you must know, that
here they live on Steams. The art of
Cookery is to shut up in great Vessels,
made on purpose, the Exhalations that
proceed from the Meat whilst it is a
dressing; and when they have provided
enough of several sorts and several
tastes, according to the Appetite of
those they treat; they open one Vessel
where that Steam is kept, and after that
another; and so on till the Company be
satisfied.

"Unless you have already lived after
this manner, you would never think,
that the Nose without Teeth and Gul-
let can perform the office of the
Mouth in feeding a Man; but I'll make

you experience it your self." He had
no sooner said so, but I found so many
agreeable and nourishing Vapours enter
the Parlour, one after another, that in
less than half a quarter of an Hour I was
fully satisfied. When we were got up;
"This is not a matter," said he, "much
to be admired at; seeing you cannot
have lived so long, and not have observed, that all sorts of Cooks, who eat
less than People of another Calling,
are neverthless much Fatter. Whence
proceeds that Plumpness, d'ye think,
unless it be from the Steams that continually environ them, which penetrate
into their Bodies and fatten them?
Hence it is, that the People of this
World enjoy a more steady and vigorous Health, by reason that their Food
hardly engenders any Excrements,
which are in a manner the original [1] of
all Diseases. You were, perhaps, surprised, that before supper you were

---

[1] *Origin. Cf.* pp. 137, 170, 174 ; and *cf.* Shakspere, *Henry IV.*, Part II.:

"It hath its original from much grief."

strip_t, since it is a Custom not practised
in your Country; but it is the fashion
of this, and for this end used, that the
Animal may be the more transpirable to
the Fumes." "Sir," answered I, "there
is a great deal of probability in what
you say, and I have found somewhat of
it my self by experience; but I must
frankly tell you, That not being able
to Unbrute my self so soon, I should
be glad to feel something that my
Teeth might fix upon:" He promised I
should, but not before next Day; "because," said he, "to Eat so soon after
your meal would breed Crudities."

After we had discoursed a little
longer, we went up to a Chamber to take
our rest; a Man met us on the top of the
Stairs, who having attentively Eyed us,
led me into a Closet where the floor was
strowed with Orange-Flowers Three
Foot thick, and my Spirit into another
filled with Gilly-Flowers and Jessamines: Perceiving me amazed at that
Magnificence, he told me they were
the Beds of the Country. In fine, we

laid our selves down to rest in our several Cells, and so soon as I had stretched
my self out upon my Flowers, by the
light of Thirty large Glow-worms shut
up in a Crystal, (being the only Candles
Charon uses,[1]) I perceived the Three or
Four Boys who had stript me before
Supper, One tickling my Feet, another
my Thighs, the Third my Flanks, and
the Fourth my Arms, and all so deli-
cately and daintily, that in less than in
a Minute I was fast asleep.

Next Morning by Sun-rising my
Spirit came into my Room and said to
me, " Now I'll be as good as my Word,
you shall breakfast this Morning more
solidly that you Supped last Night."
With that I got up, and he led me by
the Hand to a place at the back of the

---

[1] " . . . On ne s'attendait guère
De voir [Charon] en cette affaire!"

In fact, our translator has made an amusing mistake, for which the printer of the 1661 edition is
perhaps partly responsible; in that edition we read :
" (Caron ne se sert pas d'autres chandelles),"
which should of course be, as in the other editions,
" Car on . . . ; " " For they use no other candles."

7

Garden, where one of the Children of the House stayed for us, with a Piece in his Hand much like to one of our Fire-Locks. He asked my Guide if I would have a dozen of Larks, because *Baboons* (one of which he took me to be,) loved to feed on them? I had hardly answered, Yes, when the Fowler discharged a Shot, and Twenty or Thirty Larks fell at our Feet ready Roasted. This, thought I presently with my self, verifies the Proverb in our World, of a Country where Larks fall ready Roasted; without doubt it has been made by some Body that came from hence. "Fall too, fall too," said my Spirit, "don't spare; for they have a knack of mingling a certain Composition with their Powder and Shot, which Kills, Plucks, Roasts, and Seasons the Fowl all at once." I took up some of them, and eat them upon his word; and to say the Truth, In all my Life time I never eat any thing so delicious.

Having thus Breakfasted we prepared to be gone, and with a Thousand odd Faces, which they use when they would shew their Love, our Landlord received a Paper from my Spirit. I asked him, if it was a Note for the Reckoning? He replied, No, that all was paid, and that it was a Copy of Verses. "How! Verses," said I, "are your Inn - Keepers here curious of Rhime then?" "It's," said he, "the Money of the Country, and the charge we have been at here, hath been computed to amount to Three *Couplets*, or Six Verses, which I have given him. I did not fear we should out-run the Constable; for though we should Pamper our selves for a whole Week, we could not spend a *Sonnet*, and I have Four about me, besides Two *Epigrams*, Two *Odes*, and an *Eclogue*."

"Would to God," said I, "it were so in our World; for I know a good many honest Poets there who are ready to Starve, and who might live plentifully if that Money would pass in Payment." I farther asked him, If these Verses would always serve, if one

Transcribed them?   He made answer,
No, and so went on: "When an Author
has Composed any, he carries them to
the Mint, where the sworn Poets of the
Kingdom sit in Court.   There these
versifying Officers essay the pieces; and
if they be judged Sterling, they are
rated not according to their Coyn;
that's to say, That a *Sonnet* is not always as good as a *Sonnet;* but according to the intrinsick value of the piece;
so that if any one Starve, he must be
a Blockhead: For Men of Wit make
always good Chear."   With Extasie I
was admiring the judicious Policy of
that Country, when he proceeded in
this manner:

"There are others who keep Publick-
house after a far different manner:
When one is about to be gone, they demand, proportionably to the Charges,
an Acquittance for the other World;
and when that is given them, they write
down in a great Register, which they
call *Doomsday's Book*, much after this
manner: *Item*, The value of so many

Verses, delivered such a Day, to such a Person, which he is to pay upon the receipt of this Acquittance, out of his readiest Cash: And when they find themselves in danger of Death, they cause these Registers to be Chopt in pieces, and swallow them down; because they believe, that if they were not thus digested, they would be good for nothing."

This Conversation was no hinderance to our Journey; for my Four-legged Porter jogged on under me, and I rid stradling on his Back. I shall not be particular in relating to you all the Adventures that happened to us on our way, till we arrived at length at the Town where the King holds his Residence.

CHAPTER IX.

Of the little Spaniard *whom he met there, and of his quaint Wit; of* Vacuum, *Specific Weights, and sundry other Philosophical Matters.*

I was no sooner come, but they carried me to the Palace, where the Grandees received me with more Moderation, than the People had done as I passed the Streets: But both great and small concluded, That without doubt I was the Female of the Queen's little Animal. My Guide was my Interpreter; and yet he himself understood not the Riddle, and knew not what to make of that little Animal of the Queen's; but we were soon satisfied as to that; for the King having some time considered me, ordered it to be brought, and about half an hour after I saw a company of Apes, wearing

Ruffs and Breeches, come in, and amongst them a little Man almost of my own Built, for he went on Two Legs; so soon as he perceived me, he Accosted me with a *Criado de vuestra merced.*[1] I answered his Greeting much in the same Terms. But alas! no sooner had they seen us talk together, but they believed their Conjecture to be true; and so, indeed, it seemed; for he of all the By-standers, that past the most favourable Judgment upon us, protested that our Conversation was a Chattering we kept for Joy at our meeting again.

That little Man told me, that he was an *European*, a Native of old *Castille:*[2] That he had found a means by the help of Birds[3] to mount up

[1] "Your excellency's servant."

[2] Domingo Gonzales, the hero of Bishop Francis Godwin's *The Man in the Moone* (see p. 4, note), who says of himself: "I must acknowledge my Stature is so little, as I think no Man living is less."

[3] The engraving opposite, showing how he was carried up by his birds, is copied from an old edition of *The Man in the Moone*. The other winged figures about him are supposed to represent

to the World of the Moon, where then we were: That falling into the Queen's Hands, she had taken him for a Monkey, because Fate would have it so, That in that Country they cloath Apes in a *Spanish* Dress; and that upon his arrival, being found in that habit, she had made no doubt but he was of the same kind. "It could not otherwise be," replied I, "but having tried all Fashions of Apparel upon them, none were found so Ridiculous, and by consequence more becoming a kind of Animals which are only entertained for Pleasure and Diversion." "That shews you little understand the Dignity of our Nation," answered he, "for whom the Universe breeds Men only to be our Slaves, and Nature produces nothing but objects of Mirth and Laughter." He then intreated me to tell him, how I durst be so bold as to Scale the Moon with the Machine I told him of? I answered, That it was be-

demons who attacked him when just above "the middle region."

THE "LITTLE SPANIARD'S" TRIP TO THE MOON.

—*From an Engraving in "The Strange Voyage of Domingo Gonzales to the World in the Moon."*

cause he had carried away the Birds, which I intended to have made use of. He smiled at this Raillery; and about a quarter of an hour after, the King commanded the Keeper of the Monkeys to carry us back.   The King's Pleasure was punctually obeyed; at which I was very glad, for the satisfaction I had, of having a Mate to converse with during the solitude of my Brutification.

One Day my Male (for I was taken for the Female) told me, That the true reason which had obliged him to travel all over the Earth, and at length to abandon it for the Moon, was that he could not find so much as one Country where even Imagination was at liberty.   "Look ye," said he, "how the Wittiest thing you can say, unless you wear a Cornered Cap, if it thwart the Principles of the Doctors of the Robe, you are an Ideot, a Fool, and something worse perhaps.   I was about to have been put into the Inquisition at home, for maintaining to the Pedants Teeth, That there was a *Vacuum*, and that I knew no one matter in the World more Ponderous than another." I asked him, what probable Arguments he had, to confirm so new an Opinion? "To evince that," answered he, "you must suppose that there is but one Element; for though we see Water, Earth, Air and Fire distinct, yet are they never found to be so perfectly pure but that there still remains some Mixture. For example, When you behold Fire, it is not Fire but Air much extended; the Air is but Water much dilated; Water is but liquified Earth, and the Earth it self but condensed Water; and thus if you weigh Matter seriously, you'll find it is but one, which like an excellent Comedian here below acts all Parts, in all sorts of Dresses: Otherwise we must admit as many Elements as there are kinds of Bodies: And if you ask me why Fire burns, and Water cools, since it is but one and the same matter, I answer, That that matter acts by Sympathy, according to the Disposition it is in at the time when it acts. Fire,

which is nothing but Earth also, more
dilated than is fit for the constitution
of Air, strives to change into it self, by
Sympathy, what ever it meets with:
Thus the heat of Coals, being the most
subtile Fire, and most proper to penetrate a Body, at first slides through the
pores of our Skin; and because it is a
new matter that fills us, it makes us
exhale in Sweat; that Sweat dilated by
the Fire is converted to a Steam, and
becomes Air; that Air being farther
rarified by the heat of the *Antiperistasis*, or of the Neighbouring Stars, is
called Fire, and the Earth abandoned
by the Cold and Humidity which were
Ligaments to the whole, falls to the
ground: Water, on the other hand,
though it no ways differ from the matter of Fire, but in that it is closer,
burns us not; because that being dense
by Sympathy, it closes up the Bodies it
meets with, and the Cold we feel is no
more but the effect of our Flesh con-
tracting it self, because of the Vicinity
of Earth or Water, which constrains it

to a Resemblance.   Hence it is, that those who are troubled with a Dropsie convert all their nourishment into Water; and the Cholerick convert all the Blood that is formed in their Liver into Choler.

"It being then supposed, that there is but one Element; it is most certain, that all Bodies, according to their several qualities, incline equally towards the Center of the Earth.   But you'll ask me, Why then does Iron, Metal, Earth and Wood, descend more swiftly to the Center than a Sponge, if it be not that it is full of Air which naturally tends upwards?   That is not at all the Reason, and thus I make it out: Though a Rock fall with greater Rapidity than a Feather, both of them have the same inclination for the Journey; but a Cannon Bullet, for instance, were the Earth pierced through, would precipitate with greater haste to the Center thereof than a Bladder full of Wind; and the reason is, because that mass of Metal is a great deal of Earth

contracted into a little space, and that
Wind a very little Earth in a large
space: For all the parts of Matter,
being so closely joined together in the
Iron, encrease their force by their
Union; because being thus compacted,
they are many that Fight against a few,
seeing a parcel of Air equal to the Bullet in Bigness is not equal in Quantity.

" Not to insist on a long Deduction of
Arguments to prove this, tell me in
good earnest, How a Pike, a Sword or
a Dagger wounds us? If it be not because the Steel, being a matter wherein
the parts are more continuous and
more closely knit together than your
Flesh is, whose Pores and Softness
shew that it contains but very little
Matter within a great extent of Place;
and that the point of the Steel that
pricks us, being almost an innumerable
number of Particles of matter against
a very little Flesh, it forces it to yeild
to the stronger, in the same manner as
a Squadron in close order will easily
break through a more open Battallion;

for why does a Bit of red hot Iron burn more than a Log of Wood all on Fire? Unless it be, that in the Iron there is more Fire in a small space, seeing it adheres to all the parts of the Metal, than in the Wood which being very Spongy by consequence contains a great deal of *Vacuity;* and that *Vacuity*, being but a Privation of Being, cannot receive the form of Fire.   But, you'll object, you suppose a *Vacuum*, as if you had proved it, and that's begging of the question: Well then I'll prove it, and though that difficulty be the Sister of the *Gordian knot*, yet my Arms are strong enough to become its *Alexander*.

"Let that vulgar Beast, then, who does not think it self a Man, had it not been told so, answer me if it can: Suppose now there be but one Matter, as I think I have sufficiently proved; whence comes it, that according to its Appetite it enlarges or contracts its self; whence is it, that a piece of Earth by being Condensed becomes a Stone?

Is it that the parts of that Stone are placed one with another, in such a manner that wherever that grain of Sand is settled, even there, or in the same point, another grain of Sand is Lodged? That cannot be, no not according to their own Principles, seeing there is no Penetration of Bodies: But that matter must have crowded together, and if you will, abridged it self, so that it hath filled some place which was empty before. To say that it is incomprehensible, that there should be a Nothing in the World, that we are in part made up of Nothing: Why not, pray? Is not the whole World wrapt up in Nothing? Since you yield me this point, then confess ingeniously, that it's as rational that the World should have a Nothing within it, as Nothing about it.

"I well perceive you'll put the question to me, Why Water compressed in a Vessel by the Frost should break it, if it be not to hinder a Vacuity? But I answer, That that only happens, because the Air overhead, which as well as Earth and Water tends to the Center, meeting with an empty Tun by the way, takes up his Lodging there: If it find the pores of that Vessel, that's to say, the ways that lead to that void place, too narrow, too long, and too crooked, with impatience it breaks through and arrives at its Tun.

"But not to trifle away time, in answering all their objections, I dare be bold to say, That if there were no *Vacuity*, there could be no Motion; or else a Penetration of Bodies must be admitted; for it would be a little too ridiculous to think, that when a Gnat pushes back a parcel of Air with its Wings, that parcel drives another before it, that other another still; and that so the stirring of the little Toe of a Flea should raise a bunch upon the Back of the Universe. When they are at a stand, they have recourse to Rarefaction: But in good earnest, How can it be when a Body is rarified, that one Particle of the Mass does recede from another Particle, without leaving an

empty Space betwixt them; must not
the two Bodies, which are just separated, have been at the same time in
the same place of this; and that so they
must have all three penetrated each
other? I expect you'll ask me, why
through a Reed, a Syringe or a Pump,
Water is forced to ascend contrary to
its inclination?   To which I answer,
That that's by violence, and that it is
not the fear of a *Vacuity* that, turns it
out of the right way; but that being
. linked to the Air by an imperceptible
Chain, it rises when the Air, to which
it is joined, is rarified.

"That's no such knotty Difficulty,
when one knows the perfect Circle
and the delicate Concatenation of the
Elements: For if you attentively consider the Slime which joines the Earth
and Water together in Marriage, you'll
find that it is neither Earth nor Water;
but the Mediator betwixt these Two
Enemies. In the same manner, the
Water and Air reciprocally send a Mist,
that dives into the Humours of both, to
8

negotiate a Peace betwixt them; and the Air is reconciled to the Fire, by means of an interposing Exhalation which Unites them."

I believe he would have proceeded in his Discourse, had they not brought us our Victuals; and seeing we were a hungry, I stopt my Ears to his discourse, and opened my Stomack to the Food they gave us.

I remember another time, when we were upon our Philosophy, for neither of us took pleasure to Discourse of mean things: "I am vexed," said he, "to see a Wit of your stamp infected with the Errors of the Vulgar. You must know then, in spight of the Pedantry of *Aristotle* with which your Schools in *France* still ring, That every thing is in every thing; that's to say, for instance, That in the Water there is Fire, in the Fire Water, in the Air Earth, and in the Earth Air: Though that Opinion makes Scholars open their Eyes as big as Sawcers, yet it is easier to prove it, than perswade it. For I

ask them, in the first place, if Water
does not breed Filth: If they deny it,
let them dig a Pit, fill it with meer Element,[1] and to prevent all blind Objections let them if they please strain it
through a Strainer, and I'll oblige my
self, in case they find no Filth therein
within a certain time, to drink up all
the Water they have poured into it:
But if they find Filth, as I make no
doubt on't; it is a convincing Argument that there is both Salt and Fire
there.   Consequentially now, to find
Water in Fire; I take it to be no difficult Task.   For let them chuse Fire,
even that which is most abstracted from
Matter, as Comets are, there is a great
deal in them still; seeing if that Unctu-
ous Humour, whereof they are engen-
dered, being reduced to a Sulphur by
the heat of the Antiperistasis which
kindles them, did not find a curb of its
Violence in the humid Cold that quali-
fies and resists it, it would spend it self

---

[1] With the *pure* element (Lat., *merus*); *i.e.*, **water
aloue** unmixed with impurities or other elements.

in a trice like Lightning. Now that there is Air in the Earth, they will not deny it; or otherwise they have never heard of the terrible Earth-quakes, that have so often shaken the Mountains of *Sicily:* Besides, the Earth is full of Pores, even to the least grains of Sand that com[pose] it. Nevertheless no Man hath as yet said, that these Hollows were filled with *Vacuity:* It will not be taken amiss then, I hope, if the Air takes up its quarters there. It remains to be proved, that there is Earth in the Air; but I think it scarcely worth my pains, seeing you are convinced of it, as often as you see such numberless Legions of Atomes fall upon your heads, as even stiffle Arithmetick.

"But let us pass from simple to compound Bodies, they'll furnish me with much more frequent Subjects; and to demonstrate that all things are in all things, not that they change into one another, as your *Peripateticks* Juggle:[1] for I will maintain to their Teeth, that

[1] Fr., gazouillent, *babble.*

the Principles mingle, separate, and
mingle again in such a manner, that
that hath been made Water by the Wise
Creator of the World, will always be
Water; I shall suppose no Maxime, as
they do, but what I prove.

"And therefore take a Billet, or any
other combustible stuff, and set Fire to
it, they'll say when it is in a Flame,
That what was Wood is now become
Fire; but I maintain the contrary, and
that there is no more Fire in it, when
it is all in Flame, than before it was
kindled; but that which before was hid
in the Billet, and by the Humidity and
Cold hindered from acting; being now
assisted by the Stranger, hath rallied
its forces against the Phlegm that
choaked it, and commanding the Field
of Battle, that was possessed by its
Enemy, triumphs over his Jaylor and
appears without Fetters. Don't you
see how the Water flees out at the two
ends of the Billet, hot and smoaking
from the Fight it was engaged in.
That flame which you see rise on high

is the purer Fire, unpestered from the
Matter, and by consequence the readiest to return home to it self: Nevertheless it Unites it self by tapering into
a Piramide till it rise to a certain
height, that it may pierce through the
thick Humidity of the Air which resists it; but as mounting it disengaged
it self by little and little from the violent company of its Landlords; so it
diffuses it self, because then it meets
with nothing that thwarts its passage,
which negligence, though, is many
times the cause of a second Captivity:
For marching stragglingly, it wanders
sometimes into a Cloud, and if it meet
there with a Party of its own sufficient
to make head against a Vapour, they
Engage, Grumble, Thunder and Roar,
and the Death of Innocents is many
times the effect of the animated Rage
of those inanimated Things. If, when
it finds it self pestered among those
Crudities of the middle Region, it is
not strong enough to make a defence,
it yields to its Enemy upon discretion;

which by its weight constrains it to fall
again to the Earth: And this Wretch,[1]
inclosed in a drop of Rain, may per
haps fall at the Foot of an Oak, whose
Animal Fire will invite the poor Strag-
gler to take a Lodging with him; and
thus you have it in the same condition
again as it was a few Days before.

"But let us trace the Fortune of the
other Elements that composed that Billet.   The Air retreats to its own Quarters also, though blended with Vapours;
because the Fire all in a rage drove
them briskly out *Pell-mell* together.
Now you have it serving the Winds for a
Tennis-ball, furnishing Breath to Animals, filling up the Vacuities that Nature hath left; and, it may be also, wrapt
up in a drop of Dew, suckling the thir-
sty Leaves of that Tree, whither our
Fire retreated: The Water driven from
its Throne by the Flame, being by the
heat elevated to the Nursery of the Meteors, will distil again in Rain upon our
Oak, as soon as upon another; and the

[1] Unfortunate creature (" ce malheureux ").

Earth being turned to Ashes, and then cured of its Sterility, either by the nourishing Heat of a Dunghill on which it hath been thrown, or by the vegetative Salt of some neighbouring Plants, or by the teeming Waters of some Rivers, may happen also to be near this Oak, which by the heat of its Germ will attract it, and convert it into a part of its bulk.

"In this manner, these Four Elements undergo the same Destiny, and return to the same State, which they quitted but a few days before: So that it may be said, that all that's necessary for the composition of a Tree, is in a Man; and in a Tree, all that's necessary for making of a Man. In fine, according to this way, all things will be found in all things; but we want a *Prometheus*, to pluck us out of the Bosom of Nature, and render us sensible, which I am willing to call the *First Matter*."[1]

[1] The translator has here mistaken a Dative for an Accusative. The sense of the French is: "But we need a Prometheus to pluck out for us, from the bosom of Nature, and make tangible to us, that which I will call *First Matter*."

These were the things, I think, with
which we past the time; for that little
Spaniard had a quaint Wit. Our conversation, however, was only in the
Night time; because from Six a clock
in the morning until night, Crowds of
the People, that came to stare at us in
our Lodging, would have disturbed us:
For some threw us Stones, others Nuts,
and others Grass; there was no talk,
but of the Kings Beasts; we had our
Victuals daily at set hours. I cannot
tell, whether it was that I minded their
Gestures and Tones more than my Male
did: But I learnt sooner than he to understand their Language, and to smatter
a little of it, which made us to be lookt
upon in another guess manner than
formerly; and the news thereupon flew
presently all over the Kingdom, that
two Wild Men had been found, who
were less than other Men, by reason of
the bad Food we had had in the Desarts; and who through a defect of their
Parents Seed, had not the fore Legs
strong enough to support their Bodies.

CHAPTER X.

Where the Author comes in doubt, whether he be a Man, *an* Ape, *or an* Estridge; [1] *and of the Opinion of the Lunar Philosophers concerning* Aristotle.

This belief would have taken rooting by being spread, had it not been for the Learned Men of the Country, who opposed it, saying, That it was horrid Impiety to believe not only Beasts, but Monsters, to be of their kind. It would be far more probable, (added the calmer Sort) that our Domestick Beasts should participate of the privilege of Humanity and by consequence of Immortality, as being bred in our Country, than a Monstrous Beast that talks of being born I know not where, in the Moon; and then observe the difference

[1] Ostrich.

betwixt us and them. We walk upon
Four Feet, because God would not trust
so precious a thing upon weaker Sup-
porters, and he was afraid least marching otherwise some Mischance might
befall Man; and therefore he took the
pains to rest him upon four Pillars,
that he might not fall, but disdaining
to have a hand in the Fabrick of these
two Brutes, he left them to the Caprice
of Nature, who not concerning her self
with the loss of so small a matter, supported them only by Two Feet.

"Birds themselves," said they, "have
not had so hard measure as they; for
they have got Feathers at least, to supply the weakness of their Legs, and to
cast themselves in the Air when we
pursue them; whereas Nature depriv-
ing these Monsters of Two Legs, hath
disabled them from scaping our Justice.

"Besides, consider a little how they
have the Head raised toward Heaven;
it is because God would punish them
with scarcity of all things, that he hath
so placed them; for that supplicant

Posture shews that they complain to Heaven of him that Created them, and that they beg Permission to make their best of our Leavings.   But we, on the contrary, have the Head bending downwards, to behold the Blessings whereof we are the Masters, and as if there were nothing in Heaven that our happy condition needed Envy."

I heard such Discourses, or the like, daily at my Lodge; and at length they so curbed the minds of the people as to that point, that it was decreed, That at best I should only pass for a Parrot without Feathers; for they confirmed those who were already perswaded, in that I had but two Legs no more than a Bird, which was the cause that I was put into a Cage by express orders from the Privy Council.

There the Queen's Bird-keeper taking the pains daily to teach me to Whistle, as they do Stares [1] or Singing-Birds here, I was really happy in that I wanted not Food: In the mean while,

[1] Starlings.

with the Sonnets[1] the Spectators stunned me [with], I learnt to speak as they did; so that when I was got to be so much Master of the Idiom as to express most of my thoughts, I told them the finest of my Conceits. The Quaintness of my Sayings was already the entertainment of all Societies, and my Wit was so much esteemed that the Council was obliged to Publish an Edict, forbidding all People to believe that I was endowed with Reason; with express Commands to all Persons, of what Quality or Condition soever, not to imagine but that whatever I did, though never so wittily, proceeded only from Instinct.

Nevertheless, the decision of what I was, divided the Town into Two Factions. The party that stood for me encreased daily; and at length in spight of the *Anathema*, whereby they endeavoured to scare the multitude: They who held for me, demanded a Convention of the States, for determin-

[1] Fr., " sornettes," *nonsense.*

ing that Controversie.   It was long before they could agree in the Choice of
those who should have a Vote; but the
Arbitrators pacified the heat, by making the number of both parties equal,
who ordered that I should be brought
unto the Assembly, as I was: But I
was treated there with all imaginable
Severity.   My Examiners, amongst
other things, put questions of Philosophy to me; I ingenuously told them
all that my Tutor had heretofore taught
me, but they easily refuted me by more
convincing Arguments: So that having nothing to answer for my self, my
last refuge was to Principles of *Aristotle*, which stood me in as little stead,
as his Sophisms did; for in two Words,
they let me see the falsity of them.

"That same Aristotle," said they,
" whose Learning you brag so much of,
did without doubt accommodate Principles to his Philosophy;[1] instead of ac-
commodating his Philosophy to Principles; and besides he ought to have

[1] Wrest the facts to fit his theories.

proved them at least to be more rational than those of the other Sects you mentioned to us: Wherefore the good Man will not take it ill, we hope, if we bid him God b'w'."

In fine, when they perceived that I did nothing but bawl, that they were not more knowing than *Aristotle*, and that I was forbid to dispute against those who denied his Principles: They all unanimously concluded, That I was not a Man, but perhaps a kind of *Estridge*,[1] seeing I carried my Head upright like them, that I walked on two Legs, and that, in short, but for a little Down, I was every way like one of them; so that the Bird-keeper was ordered to have me back to my Cage. I spent my time pretty pleasantly there, for because I had correctly learned their Language, the whole Court took pleasure to make me prattle. The Queen's Maids, among the rest, slipt always some Boon into my Basket, and the gentilest of them all, having conceived

[1] Ostrich.

some kindness for me, was so transported with Joy, when in private I entertained her with the manners and divertisements of the People of our World, and especially our Bells, and other Instruments of Musick, that she protested to me, with Tears in her Eyes, That if ever I found my self in a condition to fly back again to our World, she would follow me with all her Heart.

CHAPTER XI.

Of the Manner of making War in the Moon; and of how the Moon is not the Moon, nor the Earth the Earth.

One Morning early, having started out of my Sleep, I found her Taboring[1] upon the grates of my Cage: "Take good heart," said she to me, "yesterday in Council a War was resolved upon, against the King ▬▬▬ [2] I hope that during the hurry of Preparations, whilst our Monarch and his Subjects are absent, I may find an occasion to make your escape." "How, a War,"

---

[1] Drumming, striking; *cf.* Nahum ii. 7: "And her maids shall lead her as with the voice of doves, tabouring upon their breasts."

[2] Cyrano writes all proper names by musical notation, in imitation of the language of the moon as he has described it.

9

said I interrupting her, "have the
Princes of this World, then, any quar-
rels amongst themselves, as those of
ours have?   Good now, let me know
their way of Fighting."

"When the Arbitrators," replied she,
"who are freely chosen by the two Parties, have appointed the time for rais-
ing Forces for their March, the number
of Combatants, the day and place of
Battle, and all with so great equality,
that there is not one Man more in one
Army, than in the other: All the
maimed Soldiers on the one side, are
lifted in one Company; and when they
come to engage, the *Mareshalls de
Camp* [1] take care to expose them to the
maimed of the other side: The Giants
are matched with Colosses, the Fencers
with those that can handle their Weap-
ons, the Valiant with the Stout, the
Weak with the Infirm, the Sick with

---

[1] Possibly "field officers" here; in exact ranking,
the Maréchal de Camp stands between Colonel and
Lieutenant-Général, and corresponds to Brigadier-
General.

the Indisposed, the Sturdy with the
Strong; and if any undertake to strike
at another than the Enemy he is
matched with, unless he can make it
out that it was by mistake, he is Condemned for a Coward.   When the Battle is over, they take an account of the
Wounded, the Dead and the Prisoners,
for Run-aways they have none; and if
the loss be equal on both sides, they
draw Cuts, who shall be Proclaimed
Victorious.

"But though a Kingdom hath de-
feated the Enemy in open War, yet
there is hardly any thing got by it; for
there are other smaller Armies of
Learned and Witty Men, on whose
Disputations the Triumph or Servitude
of States wholly depends.

"One Learned Man grapples with
another, one Wit with another, and one
Judicious Man with another Judicious
Man: Now the Triumph which a State
gains in this manner is reckoned as good
as three Victories by open force.   After
the Proclamation of Victory, the Assem-

bly is broken up, and the Victorious People either chuse the Enemies King to be theirs, or confirm their own."

I could not forbear to Laugh at this scrupulous way of giving Battle; and for an Example of much stronger Politicks, I alledged the Customs of our *Europe*, where the Monarch would be sure not to let slip any favourable occasion of gaining the day; but mind what she said as to that.

"Tell me, pray, if your Princes use not a pretext of Right, when they levy Arms:" "No doubt," answered I, "and of the Justice of their Cause too." "Why then," replied she, "do they not chuse Impartial and Unsuspected Arbitrators to compose their Differences? And if it be found, that the one has as much Right as the other, let things continue as they were; or let them play a game at *Picket*, for the Town or Province that's in dispute."

"But why all these Circumstances," replied I, "in your way of Fighting? Is it not enough, that both Armies are

equal in the number of Men?" "Your
Judgment is Weak," answered she.
"Would you think in Conscience, that
if you had the better of your Enemy,
Hand to Hand, in an open Field, you
had fairly overcome him, if you had
had on a Coat of Mail, and he none; if
he had had but a Dagger, and you a
Tuck[1]; and in a Word, if he had had
but one Arm, and you both yours?
Nevertheless, what Equality soever
you may recommend to your Gladia-
tors, they never fight on even terms;
for the one will be a tall Man, and the
other Short; the one skilful at his weapon, and the other a Man that never
handled a Sword; the one will be
strong, and the other Weak: And
though these Disproportions were not,
but that the one were as skillful and
strong as the other; yet still they
might not be rightly matched; for one,
perhaps, may have more Courage than
the other, who being rash and hot-

[1] Fencing sword. *Cf*. Shakspere, *Hamlet:*
"If he by chance escape your venomed tuck."

headed, inconcerned in danger, as not foreseeing it; of a bilious Temper, a more contracted Heart, with all the qualities that constitute Courage, (as if that, as well as a Sword, were not a Weapon which his Adversary hath not:) He makes nothing of falling desperately upon, terrifying, and killing this poor Man, who foresees the danger; who has his Heat choked in Phlegme, and a Heart too wide to close in the Spirits in such a posture as is necessary for thawing that Ice which is called Cowardise. And now you praise that Man, for having killed his Enemy at odds, and praising him for his Boldness you praise him for a Sin against nature; seeing such Boldness tends to its destruction. And this puts me in mind to tell ye, that some Years ago application was made to the Council of War for a more circumspect and conscientious Rule to be made, as to the way of Fighting. The Philosopher who gave the advice, if I mistake it not, spake in this manner.

" ' You imagine, Gentlemen, that you have very equally balanced the advantages of two Enemies, when you have chosen both Tall Men, both skillful, and both couragious: But that's not enough, seeing after all the Conquerour must have the better on't either through his Skill, Strength, or good Fortune. If it be by Skill, without doubt he hath taken his Adversary on the blind side, which he did not expect; or struck him sooner than was likely, or faining to make his Pass on one side, he hath attacked him on the other: Nevertheless all this is Cunning, Cheating, and Treachery, and none of these make a brave Man: If he hath triumphed by Force, would you judge his Enemy over-come, because he hath been over-powered? No; doubtless, no more than you'll say that a Man hath lost the Victory, when, over-whelm'd by a Mountain, it was not in his power to gain it: Even so, the other was not overcome, because he was not in a suitable Disposition, at that nick of time, to resist the violences of his Adversary. If Chance hath given him the better of his Enemy, Fortune ought then to be Crowned, since he hath contributed nothing to it; and, in fine, the vanquished is no more to be blamed, than he who at Dice having thrown Seventeen, is beat by another that throws three Sixes. '

" They confessed he was in the right; but that it was impossible, according to humane Appearances, to remedy it; and that it was better to submit to a small inconvenience, than to open a door to a hundred of greater Importance."

She entertained me no longer at that time, because she was afraid to be found alone with me so early; not that Impudicity is a Crime in that Country: On the contrary, except Malefactors Convicted, all Men have power over all Women; and in the same manner, a Woman may bring her Action against a Man for refusing her: But she durst not keep me company publickly, because the Members of Council, at their last meeting, had said, That it was chiefly the Women who gave it out that I was a Man; which was the reason that for a long time I neither saw her, nor any other of her Sex.

In the mean time, some must needs have revived the Disputes about the Definition of my Being; for whilst I was thinking of nothing else but of dying in my Cage, I was once more brought out to have another Audience. I was then questioned, in presence of a great many Courtiers, upon some points of Natural Philosophy; and, as I take it, my Answers gave some kind of Satisfaction; for the President declared to me at large his thoughts concerning the structure of the World. They seemed to me very ingenious; and had he not traced it to its Original,[1] which he maintained to be Eternal, I should have thought his Philosophy[2] more rational than our own: But as soon as I heard him maintain a Foppery[2] so contrary to

[1] *Cf.* p. 95, n. 1.
[2] Folly, foolishness, ridiculous belief. *Cf.* Shak-

. our Faith, I broke with him; at which he did but laugh; and that obliged me to tell him, That since they were thereabouts with it, I began again to think that their World was but a Moon.

But then all cried, "Don't you see here Earth, Rivers, Seas? what's all that then?" "No matter," said I, "*Aristotle* assures us it is but a Moon; and if you had said the contrary in the Schools, where I have been bred, you would have been hissed at." At this they all burst out in laughter; you need not ask, if it was their Ignorance that made them do so; for in the mean time I was carried back to my Cage.

But some more passionate Doctors, being informed that I had the boldness to affirm, That the Moon, from whence I came, was a World; and that their World was no more but a Moon, thought it might give them a very just pretext to have me condemned to the

spere. *Merry Wives of Windsor:* ". . . drove the grossness of the *foppery* into a received belief."

Water, for that's their way of rooting
out Hereticks. For that end, they
went in a Body, and complained to the
King, who promised them Justice; and
order'd me once more to be brought to
the Bar.

Now was I the third time Un-caged;
and then the most Ancient spoke, and
pleaded against me. I do not well remember his Speech; because I was too
much frighted to receive the tones of
his Voice without disorder; and because also in declaiming, he made use
of an Instrument which stunn'd me
with its noise: It was a Speaking-
Trumpet, which he had chosen on purpose that by its Martial Sound he might
rouse them to my death; and by that
Emotion of their Spirits, hinder Reason from performing its Office: As it
happens in our Armies, where the noise
of Drums and Trumpets hinders the
Souldiers from minding the importance
of their Lives.

When he had done, I rose up to defend my Cause; but I was excused from

it, by an Accident that will surprize
you.   Just as I had opened my Mouth,
a Man, who with much ado had pressed
through the Crowd, fell at the King's
Feet, and a long while rouled himself
upon his Back in his presence.   This
practice did not at all surprize me, because I knew it to be the posture they
put themselves into, when they have a
mind to be heard in publick: I only stopt
my own Harangue, and gave Ear to his.
"Just Judges," said he, "listen to
me; you cannot Condemn that Man,
that Monkey or Parrot, for saying,
That the Moon from whence he comes
is a World; for if he be a Man, though
he were not come from the Moon, since
all Men are free, is not he free also to
imagine what he pleases?   How can
you constrain him not to have Visions,
as well as you?   You may very well
force him to say, That the Moon is not
a World, but he will not believe it for
all that; for to believe a thing, some pos-
sibilities enclining more to the Yea than
to the Nay, must offer to ones Imagina-

tion: And unless you furnish him with that Probability, or his own mind hit upon it, he may very well tell you that he believes, but still remain an Infidel.[1]

"I am now to prove, that he ought not to be condemned if you lift him in the Catalogue of Beasts.

"For suppose him to be an Animal without Reason, would it be rational in you to Condemn him for offending against it? He hath said, that the Moon is a World. Now Beasts act only by the instinct of Nature: it is Nature then that says so, and not he: To think that wise Nature, who hath made the World and the Moon, knows not her self what it is; and that ye who have no more Knowledge but what ye derive from her, should more certainly know it, would be very Ridiculous. But if Passion should make you renounce your Principles, and you should suppose that Nature does not guide Beasts;

[1] *Cf.* the saying attributed to Galileo immediately after his public recantation (June 22, 1633): " E pur si muove "—" yet it does move."

blush, at least, to think on't, that the
Caprices of a Beast should so discom-
pose you.

"Really, Gentlemen, should you
meet with a Man come to the Years of
Discretion, who made it his business to
inspect the Government of *Pismires*,
giving a blow to one that had over-
thrown its Companion, imprisoning
another that had robb'd its Neighbour
of a grain of Corn, and inditing a third
for leaving its Eggs; would you not
think him a mad Man, to be employed
in things so far below him, and to pre-
tend to give Laws to Animals, that
never had Reason? How will you then,
most Venerable Assembly, justifie your
selves for being so concerned at the
Caprices of that little Animal? Just
Judges, I have no more to say."

When he had made an end, all the
Hall rung again with a kind of Musical
Applause; and after all the Opinions
had been canvased, during the space
of a large quarter of an hour, the King
gave Sentence:

That for the future, I should be re-
puted to be a Man, accordingly set at
liberty, and that the Punishment of
being Drowned, should be converted
into a publick Disgrace (the most honourable way of satisfying the Law in
that Country) whereby I should be
obliged to retract openly what I had
maintained in saying, That the Moon
was a World, because of the Scandal
that the novelty of that opinion might
give to weak Brethren.

This Sentence being pronounced, I
was taken away out of the Palace, richly
Cloathed; but in derision, carried in a
magnificent Chariot, as on a Tribunal,
which four Princes in Harness drew;
and in all the publick places of the
Town, I was forced to make this Dec-
laration:

"Good People, I declare to you, That
this Moon here is not a Moon, but a
World; and that that World below is
not a World, but a Moon: This the
Council thinks fit you should believe."

CHAPTER XII.

Of a Philosophical Entertainment.

After I had Proclaimed this, in the five great places of the Town, my Advocate came and reached me his Hand to help me down. I was in great amaze, when after I had Eyed him I found him to be my Spirit; we were an hour in embracing one another: "Come lodge with me," said he, "for if you return to Court, after a Publick Disgrace, you will not be well lookt upon: Nay more, I must tell you, that you would have been still amongst the Apes yonder, as well as the *Spaniard* your Companion, if I had not in all Companies published the vigour and force of your Wit, and gained from your Enemies the protection of the great Men in your favours." I ceased not to thank him all the way, till we came to his Lodgings;

there he entertained me till Supper-
time with all the Engines he had set
a work to prevail with my Enemies,
notwithstanding the most specious
pretexts they had used for riding the
Mobile,[1] to desist from so unjust a Pros-
ecution.   But as they came to acquaint
us that Supper was upon the Table, he
told me that to bear me company that
evening he had invited Two Professors
of the University of the Town to Sup
with him: " I'll make them," said he,
" fall upon the Philosophy which they
teach in this World, and by that means
you shall see my Landlord's Son: He's
as Witty a Youth as ever I met with;
he would prove another *Socrates*, if he
could use his Parts aright, and not
bury in Vice the Graces wherewith God
continually visits him, by affecting a
Libertinism,[2] as he does, out of a Chi-

---

[1] The people, the populace. *Cf.* pp. 74 and 168.
[2] " Libertinism " in seventeenth-century English
is like the French *libertinage*, applied rather to
licentiousness of opinion than of practice; so here
it means rather " free thought " than free living.

10

merical Ostentation and Affectation of the name of a Wit. I have taken Lodgings here, that I may lay hold on all Opportunities of Instructing him:" He said no more, that he might give me the Liberty to speak, if I had a mind to it; and then made a sign, that they should strip me of my disgraceful Ornaments, in which I still glistered.

The Two Professors, whom we expected, entered just as I was undrest, and we went to sit down to Table, where the Cloth was laid, and where we found the Youth he had mentioned to me, fallen to already. They made him a low Reverence, and treated him with as much respect as a Slave does his Lord. I asked my Spirit the reason of that, who made me answer, that it was because of his Age; seeing in that World, the Aged rendered all kind of Respect and Difference [1] to the Young; and which is far more, that the Parents obeyed their Children, so soon as by the Judgment of the Senate of Philos-

[1] Deference.

ophers they had attained to the Years
of Discretion.[1]

"You are amazed," continued he,
"at a Custom so contrary to that of
your Country; but it is not all repug-
nant to Reason: For say, in your Conscience, when a brisk young Man is at
his Prime in Imagining, Judging, and
Acting, is not he fitter to govern a
Family than a Decrepit piece of Threescore Years, dull and doting, whose
Imagination is frozen under the Snow
of Sixty Winters, who follows no other
Guide but what you call the Experience
of happy Successes; which yet are no
more but the bare effects of Chance,
against all the Rules and Oeconomy of
humane Prudence? And as for Judgment, he hath but little of that neither,
though the people of your World make
it the Portion of Old Age: But to undeceive them, they must know, That
that which is called Prudence in an Old
Man is no more but a panick Apprehension, and a mad Fear of acting any

[1] *Cf.* Gulliver's Voyage to Lilliput, chap. vi.

thing where there is danger: So that
when he does not run a Risk, wherein
a Young Man hath lost himself; it is
not that he foresaw the Catastrophe,
but because he had not Fire enough to
kindle those noble Flashes, which make
us dare: Whereas the Boldness of
that Young Man was as a pledge of
the good Success of his design; because
the same Ardour that speeds and facil-
itates the execution, thrust him upon
the undertaking.

"As for Execution, I should wrong
your Judgment if I endeavoured to
convince it by proofs: You know that
Youth alone is proper for Action; and
were you not fully perswaded of this,
tell me, pray, when you respect a Man
of Courage, is it not because he can re-
venge you on your Enemies or Oppres-
sors? And does any thing, but meer
Habit, make you consider [1] him, when a
Battalion of Seventy *Januarys* hath frozen his Blood and chilled all the noble
Heats that youth is warmed with?

[1] Respect.

When you yeild to the Stronger, is it
not that he should be obliged to you for
a Victory which you cannot Dispute
him? Why then should you submit to
him, when Laziness hath softened his
Muscles, weakened his Arteries, evapo-
rated his Spirits, and suckt the Marrow
out of his Bones? If you adore a
Woman, is it not because of her Beauty?
Why should you then continue your
Cringes, when Old Age hath made her
a Ghost, which only represents a hide-
ous Picture of Death? In short, when
you loved a Witty Man, it was because
by the Quickness of his Apprehension
he unravelled an intricate Affair, sea-
soned the choicest Companies with his
quaint Sayings, and sounded the depth
of Sciences with a single Thought; and
do you still honour him, when his worn
Organs disappoint his weak Noddle,
when he is become dull and uneasy in
Company, and when he looks like an
aged Fairy [1] rather than a rational Man?

[1] Fr., *Dieu Foyer*. The change seems to be an in-
teresting embroidery of the translator's fancy,

"Conclude then from thence, Son, that it is fitter Young Men should govern Families, than Old; and the rather, that according to your own Principles, *Hercules*, *Achilles*, *Epaminondas*, *Alexander*, and *Cæsar*, of whom most part died under Fourty Years of Age, could have merited no Honours, as being too Young in your account, though their Youth was the only cause of their Famous Actions; which a more advanced Age would have rendered ineffectual, as wanting that Heat and Promptitude that rendered them so highly successful. But you'll tell me, that all the Laws of your World do carefully enjoin the Respect that is due to Old Men: That's true; but it is as true also, that all who made Laws have been Old Men, who feared that Young Men might justly have dispossessed them of the Authority they had usurped.

"You owe nothing to your mortal Architector, but your Body only; your

since he has correctly translated the words as "Household God" on p. 76.

Soul comes from Heaven, and Chance might have made your Father your Son, as now you are his. Nay, are you sure he hath not hindered you from Inheriting a Crown? Your Spirit left Heaven, perhaps with a design to animate the King of the *Romans*, in the Womb of the Empress; it casually encountered the *Embryo* of you by the way, and it may be to shorten its journey, went and lodged there: No, no, God would never have razed your name out of the List of Mankind, though your Father had died a Child. But who knows, whether you might not have been at this day the work of some valiant Captain, that would have associated you to his Glory, as well as to his Estate. So that, perhaps, you are no more indebted to your Father for the life he hath given you, than you would be to a Pirate who had put you in Chains, because he feeds you: Nay, grant he had begot you a Prince, or King; a Present loses its merit, when it is made without the Option of him

who receives it.   *Cæsar* was killed, and
so was *Cassius* too: In the mean time
Cassius was obliged to the Slave, from
whom he begg'd his Death, but so was
not *Cæsar* to his Murderers, who forced
it upon him.   Did your Father consult
your Will and Pleasure, when he Em-
braced your Mother?   Did he ask you,
if you thought fit to see that Age, or to
wait for another; if you would be satisfied to be the Son of a Sot, or if you
had the Ambition to spring from a
Brave Man?   Alas, you whom alone the
business concerned, were the only Person not consulted in the case.   May be
then, had you been shut up any where
else, than in the Womb of Nature's
Ideas, and had your Birth been in your
own Opinion, you would have said to
the *Parca*, my dear Lady, take another
Spindle in your Hand: I have lain
very long in the Bed of Nothing, and I
had rather continue an Hundred years
still without a Being, than to Be to day,
that I may repent of it to morrow:
However, Be you must, it was to no

purpose for you to whimper and squall
to be taken back again to the long and
darksome House they drew you out of,
they made as if they believed you
cryed for the Teat.

"These are the Reasons, at least
some of them, my Son, why Parents
bear so much respect to their Children:
I know very well that I have inclined
to the Childrens side more than in justice I ought; and that in favour of
them, I have spoken a little against my
Conscience. But since I was willing
to repress the Pride of some Parents,
who insult over the weakness of their
little Ones; I have been forced to do as
they do who to make a crooked Tree
streight bend it to the contrary side,
that betwixt two Conversions it may
become even: Thus I have made Fathers restore to their Children what
they have taken from them, by taking
from them a great deal that belonged
to them; that so another time they may
be content with their own. I know
very well also that by this Apology I

have offended all Old men: But let
them remember, that they were Children before they were Fathers, and
Young before they were Old; and that
I must needs have spoken a great deal
to their advantage, seeing they were
not found in a Parsley-bed:[1] But, in
fine, fall back, fall edge, though my
Enemies draw up against my Friends,
it will go well enough still with me; for
I have obliged all men, and only dis-
obliged but one half."

With that he held his tongue, and our
Landlord's Son spoke in this manner:
"Give me leave," said he to him,
"since by your care I am informed of the
Original, History, Customs, and Philosophy, of the World of this little Man;
to add something to what you have said;
and to prove that Children are not

---

[1] Fr., "sous une pomme de chou"—under a cab-
bage-head; where, as too curious children are sometimes told in France, the babies are found. The
English expression is exactly equivalent. *Cf.*
Locke: "Sempronia dug Titus out of the parsley
bed, as they used to tell children, and so became
his mother."

obliged to Parents for their Generation, because their Parents were obliged in Conscience to procreate them.

"The strictest Philosophy of their World acknowledges that it is better to dye, since to dye one must have lived, than not to have had a Being. Now seeing, by not giving a Being to that Nothing, I leave it in a state worse than Death, I am more guilty in not producing, than in killing it. In the mean time, my little Man, thou wouldst think thou hadst committed an unpardonable Parracide, shouldst thou have cut thy Sons throat: It would indeed be an enormous Crime, but it is far more execrable, not to give a Being to that which is capable of receiving it: For that Child whom thou deprivest of life for ever, hath had the satisfaction of having enjoyed it for some time. Besides, we know that it is but deprived of it, but for some ages; but these forty poor little Nothings, which thou mightest have made forty good Souldiers for the King, thou art so malicious as to deny them Life, and lettest them corrupt in thy Reins, to the danger of an Appoplexy, which will stifle thee."

This Philosophy did not at all please me, which made me three or four times shake my head; but our Preceptor held his tongue, because Supper was mad to be gone.

We laid our selves along, then, upon very soft Quilts, covered with large Carpets; and a young man that waited on us, taking the oldest of our Philosophers, led him into a little parlour apart, where my Spirit called to him to come back to us as soon as he had supped.

This humour of eating separately, gave me the curiosity of asking the Cause of it: "He'll not relish," said he, "the steam of Meat, nor yet of Herbs, unless they die of themselves, because he thinks they are sensible of Pain." "I wonder not so much," replied I, "that he abstains from Flesh, and all things that have had a sensitive Life: For in our World the *Pythago-*

reans, and even some holy *Anchorites*, have followed that Rule; but not to dare, for instance, cut a Cabbage, for fear of hurting it; that seems to me altogether ridiculous." "And for my part," answered my Spirit, "I find a great deal of probability in his Opinion. "For tell me, Is not that Cabbage you speak of, a Being existent in Nature, as well as you? Is not she the common Mother of you both? Yet the Opinion that Nature is kinder to Mankind, than to Cabbage-kind, tickles and makes us laugh: But seeing she is incapable of Passion, she can neither love nor hate any thing; and were she susceptible of Love, she would rather bestow her affection upon this Cabbage, which you grant cannot offend her, than upon that Man who would destroy her, if it lay in his power.

"And moreover, Man cannot be born Innocent, being a Part of the first Offendor: But we know very well, that the first Cabbage did not offend its Creator. If it be said, that we are made after the Image of the Supreme Being, and so is not the Cabbage; grant that to be true; yet by polluting our Soul, wherein we resembled Him, we have effaced that Likeness, seeing nothing is more contrary to God than Sin. If then our Soul be no longer his Image, we resemble him no more in our Feet, Hands, Mouth, Forehead and Ears, than a Cabbage in its Leaves, Flowers, Stalk, Pith, and Head: Do not you really think, that if this poor Plant could speak, when one cuts it, it would not say, ' Dear Brother Man, what have I done to thee that deserves Death? I never grow but in Gardens, and am never to be found in desart places, where I might live in Security: I disdain all other company but thine; and scarcely am I sowed in thy Garden, when to shew thee my Good-will, I blow, stretch out my Arms to thee; offer thee my Children in Grain; and as a requital for my civility, thou causest my Head to be chopt off.' Thus would a Cabbage discourse, if it could speak.

"Well, and because it cannot complain, may we therefore justly do it all
the Wrong which it cannot hinder? If
I find a Wretch bound Hand and Foot,
may I lawfully kill him, because he
cannot defend himself? so far from
that, that his Weakness would aggra-
vate my Cruelty. And though this
wretched Creature be poor, and destitute of all the advantages which we
have, yet it deserves not Death; and
when of all the Benefits of a Being it
hath only that of Encrease, we ought
not cruelly to snatch that away from it.
To massacre a Man, is not so great Sin,
as to cut and kill a Cabbage, because
one day the Man will rise again, but the
Cabbage has no other Life to hope for:
By putting to death a Cabbage, you an-
nihilate it; but in killing a Man, you
make him only change his Habitation:
Nay, I'll go farther with you still:
since God doth equally cherish all his
Works, and hath equally divided the
Benefits betwixt Us and Plants, it is
but just we should have an equal Es-

teem for Them as for our Selves.   It is
true we were born first, but in the
Family of God there is no Birth-right.
If then the Cabbage share not with us
in the inheritance of Immortality, without doubt that Want was made up by
some other Advantage, that may make
amends for the shortness of its Being;
may be by an universal Intellect, or a
perfect Knowledge of all things in their
Causes; and it's for that Reason, that
the wise Mover of all things hath not
shaped for it Organs like ours, which
are proper only for a simple Reasoning,
not only weak, but many times falla-
cious too; but others, more ingeniously
framed, stronger, and more numerous,
which serve to manage its Speculative
Exercises.   You'll ask me, perhaps,
when ever any Cabbage imparted those
lofty Conceptions to us?   But tell me,
again, who ever discovered to us certain Beings, which we allow to be above
us; to whom we bear no Analogy nor
Proportion, and whose Existence it is
as hard for us to comprehend, as the

Understanding and Ways whereby a
Cabbage expresses its self to its like,
though not to us, because our senses
are too dull to penetrate so far.

" *Moses*, the greatest of Philosophers,
who drew the Knowledge of Nature
from the Fountain-Head, Nature her
self, hinted this truth to us when he
spoke of the Tree of Knowledge; and
without doubt he intended to intimate
to us under that Figure, that Plants, in
Exclusion to Mankind, possess perfect
Philosophy. Remember, then, O thou
Proudest of Animals! that though a
Cabbage which thou cuttest sayeth not
a Word, yet it pays it at Thinking; but
the poor Vegetable has no fit Organs
to howl as you do, nor yet to frisk
it about, and weep: Yet, it hath those
that are proper to complain of the
Wrong you do it, and to draw a Judgement from Heaven upon you for the
Injustice. But if you still demand of
me, how I come to know that Cabbage
and Coleworts conceive such pretty
Thoughts? Then will I ask you, how

come you to know that they do not;
and that some amongst them, when
they shut up at Night, may not Compliment one another as you do, saying:
Good Night, Master *Cole-Curled-Pate*;
your most humble Servant, good Master *Cabbage-Round-Head*."

So far was he gone on in his Discourse, when the young Lad, who had
led out our Philosopher, led him in
again; "What, Supped already?" cryed
my Spirit to him.   He answered, yes,
almost: The Physiognomist having
permitted him to take a little more with
us.   Our young Landlord stayed not
till I should ask him the meaning of
that Mystery; "I perceive," said he,
"you wonder at this way of Living;
know then, that in your World, the
Government of Health is too much
neglected, and that our Method is not
to be despised.

"In all Houses there is a Physiognomist entertained by the Publick,[1] who
in some manner resembles your Physi-

---

[1] Supported by the State.   *Cf.* p. 34, n. 1.

cians, save that he only prescribes to
the Healthful, and judges of the different manners how we are to be Treated
only according to the Proportion, Figure, and Symetry of our Members; by
the Features of the Face, the Complex-
ion, the Softness of the Skin, the Agil-
ity of the Body, the Sound of the
Voice, and the Colour, Strength, and
Hardness of the Hair.   Did not you
just now mind a Man, of a pretty low
Stature, who ey'd you; he was the
Physiognomist of the House: Assure
your self, that according as he observed
your Constitution, he hath diversified
the Exhalation of your Supper: Mark
the Quilt on which you lie, how distant
it is from our Couches; without doubt,
he judges your Constitution to be far
different from ours; since he feared
that the Odour which evaporates from
those little Pipkins that stand under our
Noses, might reach you, or that yours
might steam to us; at Night, you'll
see him chuse the Flowers for your
Bed with the same Circumspection."

CHAPTER XIII.

Of the little Animals that make up our Life, and likewise cause our Diseases; and of the Disposition of the Towns in the Moon.

During all this Discourse, I made Signs to my Landlord, that he would try if he could oblige the Philosophers to fall upon some head of the Science which they professed. He was too much my Friend, not to start an Occasion upon the Spot: But not to trouble the Reader with the Discourse and Entreaties that were previous to the Treaty, wherein Jest and Earnest were so wittily interwoven, that it can hardly be imitated; I'll only tell you that the Doctor, who came last, after many things, spake as follows:

"It remains to be proved, that there nfinite Worlds, in an infinite

World: Fancy to your self then the
Universe as a great Animal; and that
the Stars, which are Worlds, are in this
great Animal, as other great Animals
that serve reciprocally for Worlds to
other Peoples; such as we, our Horses,
&c.   That we in our turns, are likewise Worlds to certain other Animals,
incomparably less than our selves, such
as Nits, Lice, Hand-worms, &c.   And
that these are an Earth to others, more
imperceptible ones; in the same manner as every one of us appears to be a
great World to these little People.
Perhaps our Flesh, Blood, and Spirits,
are nothing else but a Contexture of
little Animals¹ that correspond, lend us
Motion from theirs, and blindly suffer
themselves to be guided by our Will,
which is their Coachman; or otherwise
conduct us, and all Conspiring together,
produce that Action which we call Life.
    " For tell me, pray, is it a hard thing
to be believed, that a Louse takes your

¹ This and the following paragraphs appear to be
an anticipation of the microbe theory.

Body for a World; and that when any
one of them travels from one of your
Ears to the other, his Companions say,
that he hath travelled the Earth from
end to end, or that he hath run from
one Pole to the other? Yes, without
doubt, those little People take your
Hair for the Forests of their Country;
the Pores full of Liquor, for Fountains;
Buboes and Pimples, for Lakes and
Ponds; Boils, for Seas; and Defluxions,
for Deluges: And when you Comb
your self, forwards, and backwards,
they take that Agitation for the Flowing and Ebbing of the Ocean. Doth
not Itching make good what I say?
What is the little Worm that causes it
but one of these little Animals, which
hath broken off from civil Society, that
it may set up for a Tyrant in its Country? If you ask me, why are they bigger than other imperceptible Crea-
tures? I ask you, why are Elephants
bigger than we? And the *Irish*-men,
than *Spaniards?*

s to the Blisters, and Scurff,

which you know not the Cause of; they
must either happen by the Corruption
of their Enemies, which these little
Blades have killed, or which the Plague
has caused by the scarcity of Food, for
which the Seditious worried one another,[1] and left Mountains of Dead Car-
cases rotting in the Field; or because
the Tyrant, having driven away on all
Hands his Companions, who by their
Bodies stopt up the Pores of ours,
hath made way out for the waterish
matter, which being extravasted out
of the Sphere of the Circulation of
our Blood, is corrupted. It may be
asked, perhaps, why a Nit, or Hand-
worm, produces so many disorders:
But that's easily conceived; for as one
Revolt begets another, so these little
People, egg'd on by the bad Example
of their Seditious Companions, aspire
severally to Sovereign Command; and
occasion every where War, Slaughter,
and Famine.

[1] Fr., "dont les Séditieux se sont gorgés"—with
which the rebels have filled their bellies.

"But you'll say, some are far less subject to Itching than others; and, nevertheless, all are equally inhabited by these little Animals, since you say they are the Cause of our Life. That's true; for we observe, that Phlegmatick People are not so much given to scratching as the Cholerick; because the People sympathizing with the Climate they inhabit, are slower in a cold Body, than those others that are heated by the temper of their Region, who frisk and stir, and cannot rest in a place: Thus a Cholerick Man is more delicate than a Phlegmatick; because being animated in many more Parts, and the Soul being the Action of these little Beasts, he is capable of Feeling in all places where these Cattle stir. Whereas the Phlegmatick Man, wanting sufficient Heat to put that stirring Mobile in Action, is sensible but in a few places.

" To prove more plainly that universal *Vermicularity*, you need but consider, when you are wounded, how the Blood runs to the Sore: Your Doctors say that it is guided by provident Nature, who would succour the parts debilitated; which might make us conclude, that, besides the Soul and Mind, there were a third intellectual Substance, that had distinct Organs and Functions: And therefore, it seems to me far more Rational to say, That these little Animals finding themselves attacked send to demand Assistance from their Neighbours, and thus, Recruits flocking in from all Parts and the Country being too little to contain so many, they either die of Hunger or are stifled in the Press. That Mortality happens when the Boil is ripe; for as an Argument that these Animals at that time are stifled, the Flesh becomes insensible: Now, if Blood - letting, which is many times ordered to divert the Fluxion, do any good, it is because, much being lost by the Orifice which these little Animals laboured to stop, they refuse their Allies Assistance, having no more Forces than is enough to defend themselves at home."

Thus he concluded, and when the second Philosopher perceived by all our Looks that we longed to hear him speak in his turn:

"Men," said he, "seeing you are curious to instruct this little Animal, (our like), in somewhat of the Science which we profess, I am now dictating a Treatise which I wish he might see, because of the Light it gives to the Understanding of our Natural Philosophy; it is an Explication of the Original[1] of the World: But seeing I am in haste to set my Bellows at work, (for to Morrow, without delay, the Town departs;) I hope you'll excuse my want of time, and I promise to satisfie you as soon as the Town is arrived at the place whither it is to go."

At these words, the Landlord's Son called his Father, to know what it was a Clock? who having answered him, that it was past Eight, he asked him in a great Rage, Why he did not give him notice at Seven, according as he had

[1] *Cf.* p. 95, n. 1.

commanded him; that he knew well enough the Houses were to be gone to Morrow; and that the City Walls were already upon their Journey? "Son," replyed the good Man, "since you sate down to Table, there is an Order published, That no House shall budg before next day:" "That's all one," answered the young Man; "you ought blindly to obey, not to examine my Orders, and only remember what I commanded you. Quick, go fetch me your Effigies:" So soon as it was brought, he took hold on't by the Arm, and Whipt it a whole quarter of an Hour: "Away you ne'er be good," continued he; "as a Punishment for your disobedience, it's my Will and Pleasure, that this day you serve for a Laughing-stock to all People; and therefore I command you, not to walk but upon two Legs, till Night." The Poor Man went out in a very mournful Condition, and the Young man excused to us his Passion.

I had much ado, though I bit my Lip, to forbear Laughing at so pleasant a Punishment; and therefore to take me off of this odd piece of Pedantick Discipline, which, without doubt, would have made me burst out at last; I prayed my Philosopher to tell me what he meant by that Journey of the Town he talked of, and if the Houses and Walls Travelled?

"Dear Stranger," answered he, "we have some Ambulatory Towns, and some Sedentary; the Ambulatory, as for instance this wherein now we are, are Built in this manner: The Architector, as you see, builds every Palace of a very light sort of Timber; supported by four Wheels underneath; in the thickness of one of the Walls he places ten large pair of Bellows, whose Snouts pass in a Horizontal Line through the upper Story, from one Pinacle to the other; so that when Towns are to be removed from one place to another, (for according to the Seasons they change the Air) every one spreads a great many Sails upon one side of the House, before the Noses of the Bellows; then having wound up a Spring to make them play, in less than Eight days time their Houses, by the continual Puffs which these Windy Monsters blow, are driven, if one pleases, an Hundred Leagues and more.

"For those which we call Sedentary, they are almost like to your Towers; save that they are of Timber, and that they have a Great and Strong Skrew or Vice in the Middle, reaching from the top to the Bottom; whereby they may be hoisted up or let down as People please. Now the Ground under neath is dugg as deep as the House is high; and it is so ordered, that so soon as the Frosts begin to chill the Air, they may sink their Houses down under Ground, where they keep themselves secure from the Severity of the Weather: But as soon as the gentle Breathings of the Spring begin to soften and qualifie the Air; they raise them above Ground again, by means of the great Skrew I told you of."

CHAPTER XIV.

Of the Original *of All Things; of* Atomes; *and of the Operation of the Senses.*

I prayed him, since he had shew'd so much goodness, and that the Town was not to part[1] till next day, that he would tell me somewhat of that Original of the World, which he had mentioned not long before; "and I promise you," said I, "that in requital, so soon as I am got back to the Moon, from whence my Governour (pointing to my Spirit) will tell you that I am come, I'll spread your Renown there,

[1] *Part* and *depart* were interchangeable in the seventeenth century. *Cf.* Shakspere, *Two Gentlemen of Verona:*

"But now he parted hence";

her hand, *King John :*

ly departed with a part" (=*given*

by relating the rare things you shall tell me: I perceive you Laugh at that promise, because you do not believe that the Moon I speak of is a World, and that I am an Inhabitant of it; but I can assure you also, that the People of that World, who take this only for a Moon, will Laugh at me when I tell them that your Moon is a World, and that there are Fields and Inhabitants in it:"

He answered only with a smile, and spake in this manner:

"Since in Ascending to the Original of this Great A L L, we are forced to run into three or four Absurdities; it is but reasonable we should follow the way wherein we may be least apt to stumble. I say then, that the first Obstacle that stops us short is the Eternity of the World; and the minds of men, not being able enough to conceive it, and being no more able to imagine, that this great Universe, so lovely and so well ordered, could have made it self, they have had their recourse to

Creation: But like to him that would leap into a River for fear of being wet with Rain, they save themselves out of the Clutches of a Dwarf, by running into the Arms of a Giant; and yet they are not safe for all that: For that Eternity which they deny the World, because they cannot comprehend it, they attribute it to God, as if he stood in need of that Present, and as if it were easier to imagine it in the one than in the other; for tell me, pray, was it ever yet conceived in Nature, how Something can be made of Nothing? Alas! Betwixt Nothing and an Atome only, there are such infinite Disproportions, that the sharpest Wit could never dive into them; therefore to get out of this inextricable Labyrinth, you must admit of a Matter Eternal with God: But you'l say to me, grant I should allow you that Eternal Matter; how could that Chaos dispose and order it self? That's the thing I am about to explain to you.

"My little Animal, after you have

mentally divided every little Visible Body, into an infinite many little invisible Bodies; you must imagine, That the infinite Universe consists only of these Atomes, which are most solid, most incorruptible, and most simple; whose Figures are partly Cubical, partly Parallelograms, partly Angular, partly Round, partly Sharp-pointed, partly Pyramidal, partly Six-cornered, and partly Oval; which act all severally, according to their Various Figures: And to shew that it is so, put a very round Ivory Bowl upon a very smooth place, and with the least touch you give it will be half a quarter of an hour before it rest: Now I say, that if it were perfectly round, as some of the Atomes I speak of are, and the Surface on which it is put perfectly smooth, it would never rest. If Art then be capable of inclining a Body to a perpetual Motion, why may we not believe that Nature can do it? It's the same with the other Figures, of which the Square requires a perpetual Rest, others an

out but the Eyes of a Man, the Fire of whose Soul makes him to see, and he will cease to see; just as our great Clock will leave off to make the Hours, if the Movements of it be broken.

"In fine, these Primary and indivisible Atomes make a Circle, whereon without difficulty move the most preplexed Difficulties of Natural Philosophy; not so much as even the very Operation of the Senses, which no Body hitherto hath been able to conceive, but I will easily explain by these little Bodies. Let us begin with the Sight. It deserves, as being the most incomprehensible, our first Essay.

[1] "It is performed then, as I imagine, when the Tunicles of the Eye, whose Pores resemble those of Glass, transmitting that fiery Dust which is called Visual Rays, the same is stopt by some opacous Matter which makes it recoil; and then, meeting in its retreat the Image of the Object that forced it

[1] Notice that the basis of this discussion is the supposition that the visual rays *start from the eye*.

back, and that Image being but an infinite number of little Bodies exhaled
in an equal Superfice from the Object
beheld, it pursues it to our Eye:
You'll not fail to Object, I know, that
Glass is an Opacous Body, and very
Compact; and that nevertheless, instead of reflecting other Bodies, it lets
them pass through: But I answer, that
the Pores of Glass are shaped in the
same Figure as those Atomes are which
pass through it; and as a Wheat-Sieve
is not proper for Sifting of Oats, nor an
Oat-Sieve to Sift Wheat; so a Box of
Deal-Board, though it be thin and lets
a sound go through it, is impenetrable
to the Sight; and a piece of Chrystal,
though transparent and pervious to the
Eye, is not penetrable to the Touch."

I could not here forbear to interrupt
him: "A great Poet and Philosopher [1] of
our World," said I, "hath after *Epicurus* and *Democritus*,[2] spoken of these

---

[1] Lucretius. .
[2] Democritus was the originator of the atomic
theory.

little Bodies, in the same manner almost as you do; and therefore, you
don't at all surprise me by that Discourse: Only tell me, I pray, as you
proceed, how, according to your Principles, you'll explain to me the manner
of drawing your Picture in a Looking-
Glass."

"That's very easie," replied he, "for
imagine with your self, that those Fires
of our Eyes, having passed through
the Glass and meeting behind it an
Opacous Body that reverberates them,
they come back the way they went;
and finding those little Bodies marching in equal Superfices upon the Glass,
they repel them to our Eyes; and our
Imagination, hotter than the other Faculties of our Soul, attracts the more
subtile, wherewith it draws our Picture
in little.

"It is as easie to conceive the Act of
Hearing, and for *Brevities* sake,. let us
only consider it in the Harmony of a
Lute, touched by the Hand of a Master.
You'll ask me, How can it be, that I

perceive at so great a distance a thing
which I do not see? Does there a
Sponge go out of my Ears, that drinks
up that Musick, and brings it back with
it again? Or does the Player beget in
my Head another little Musician, with
another little Lute, who has Orders
like an Eccho to sing over to me the
same Airs? No; But that Miracle proceeds from this, that the String touched,
striking those little Bodies of which
the Air is composed, drives it gently
into my Brain, with those little Corporeal Nothings that sweetly pierce into
it; and according as the String is
stretched, the Sound is high, because it
more vigorously drives the Atomes;
and the Organ being thus penetrated,
furnisheth the Fancy wherewith to
make a Representation; if too little,
then our Memory not having as yet finished its Image, we are forced to repeat
the same sound to it again; to the end it
may take enough of Materials, which, for
Instance, the Measures of a *Saraband*[1]

[1] A lively Spanish dance-measure.

furnish it with, for finishing the Picture of that *Saraband ;* but that Operation is nothing near so wonderful as those others, which by the help of the same Organ excite us sometimes to Joy, sometimes to Anger.

"And this happens, when in that motion these little Bodies meet with other little Bodies within us moving in the same manner, or whose Figure renders them susceptible of the same Agitation; for then these New-comers stir up their Landlords to move as they do; & thus, when a violent Air meets with the Fire of our Blood, it inclines it to the same Motion, and animates it to a Sally, which is the thing we call Heat of Courage; if the Sound be softer, and have only force enough to raise a less Flame in greater Agitation, by leading it along the Nerves, Membranes, and through the interstices of our Flesh it excites that Tickling which is called Joy: And so it happens in the Ebullition of the other Passions, according as these little Bodies are more or less vio-

lently tossed upon us, according to the
Motion they receive by the rencounter
of other Agitations, and according as
they find Dispositions in us for motion.
So much for Hearing.

"Now, I think the Demonstration of
Touching will be every whit as easie,
if we conceive that out of all palpable
Matter there is a perpetual Emission of
little Bodies, and that the more we
touch them, the more evaporates; because we press them out of the Subject
it self, as Water out of a Sponge when
we squeez it. The Hard make a report
to the Organ of their Hardness; the
Soft, of their Softness; the Rough, &c.
And since this is so, we are not so
quaint in Feeling with Hands used to
Labour, because of the Thickness of
the Skin, which being neither porous,
nor animated, with difficulty transmits
the Evaporations of Matter. Some,
perhaps, may desire to know where the
Organ of Touching has its Residence.
For my part, I think it is spread over
all the Surface of the Body, seeing in

all parts it feels: Yet I imagine, that the nearer the Member, wherewith we touch, be to the Head, the sooner we distinguish; which Experience convinces us of, when with shut Eyes we handle any thing, for then we'll more easily guess what it is; and if on the contrary we feel it with our hinder Feet, it will be harder for us to know it: And the Reason is, because our Skin being all over perforated, our Nerves, which are of no compacter Matter, lose by the way a great many of those little Atomes through the little Holes of their Contexture, before they reach the Brain, which is their Journeys end: It remains, that I speak of the Smelling and Tasting.

"Pray tell me, when I taste a Fruit, is it not because the Heat of my Mouth melts it? Confess to me then, that there being Salts in a Pear, and that they being separated by Dissolution into little Bodies of a different Figure from those which make the Taste of an Apple; they must needs pierce our

Pallate in a very different manner: Just so as the thrust of a Pike, that passes through me, is not like the Wound which a Pistol-Bullet makes me feel with a sudden start; and as that Pistol Bullet makes me suffer another sort of Pain than that of a Slug of Steel.

"I have nothing to say, as to the Smelling, seeing the Philosophers themselves confess, that it is performed by a continual Emission of little Bodies.

" Now upon the same Principle will I explain to you the Creation, Harmony, and Influence of the Celestial Globes, with the immutable Variety of Meteors. "

He was about to proceed; but the Old Landlord coming in, made our Philosopher think of withdrawing: He brought in Christals full of Glow-worms, to light the Parlour; but seeing those little fiery Insects lose much of their Light, when they are not fresh gathered, these which were ten days old had hardly any at all. My Spirit stayed not till the Company should complain of it, but went up to his Chamber, and came immediately back again with two Bowls of Fire so Sparkling that all·wondred he burnt not his Fingers. "These incombustible Tapers," said he, "will serve us better than your Week¹ of Worms. They are Rays of the Sun, which I have purged from their Heat; otherwise, the corrosive qualities of their Fire would have dazled and offended your Eyes; I have fixed their Light, and inclosed it within these transparent Bowls.² That ought not to afford you any great Cause of Admiration; for it is not harder for me, who am a Native of the Sun, to condense his Beams, which are the Dust of that World, than it is for you

---

¹ Wick (cf. the Standard Dictionary). Some modern French editions have "pelotons de verre," meaning "glass bulbs," but this is evidently a mistake, since the seventeenth-century editions have *verres*, which is their form, in all cases, for the modern *vers*. See also the first meaning of *peloton* in Littré.

² The incandescent electric light?

to gather the Atomes of the pulveriz'd
Earth of this World."

Thereupon our Landlord sent a Servant to wait upon the Philosophers
home, it being then Night, with a dozen
Globes of Glowworms hanging at his
four Legs.   As for my Preceptor and
my self, we went to rest, by order of the
Phisiognomist.   He laid me that Night
in a Chamber of Violets and Lillies,
[and] ordered me to be tickled after
the usual manner.

CHAPTER XV.

Of the Books *in the Moon, and their Fashion; of Death, Burial, and Burning; of the Manner of telling the Time; and of* Noses.

Next Morning about Nine a Clock, my Spirit came in, and told me that he was

come from Court, where ,

one of the Queens Maids of Honour, had sent for him, and that she had enquired after me, protesting that she still persisted in her Design to be as good as her Word; that is, that with all her Heart she would follow me, if I would take her along with me to the other World; "which exceedingly pleased me," said he, "when I understood that the chief Motive which inclined her to the Voyage, was to be-

THE AUTHOR'S FLYING MACHINE.

—From a 17th Century Engraving.

give you this, which I esteem much more; it is the great Work of the Philosophers, composed by one of the greatest Wits of the Sun.[1] He proves in it that all things are true, and shews the way of uniting Physically the Truths of every Contradiction; as, for Example, That White is Black, and Black White; that one may be, and not be at the same time; that there may be a Mountain without a Valley; that nothing is something, and that all things that are, are not; but observe, that he proves all these unheard-of Paradoxes without any Captious or Sophistical Argument.

"When you are weary of Reading, you may Walk, or Converse with our Landlord's Son, he has a very Charming Wit; but that which I dislike in him is, that he is a little Atheistical. If he chance to Scandalize you, or by

have let the wind into a cedar coffer, then rarified the imprisoned element by means of cunningly adjusted burning glasses, and soared up with it."

[1] Probably Campanella; *cf.* p. 78, n. 1. On his "great work," *cf.* also p. 79, n. 1.

any Argument shake your Faith, fail not immediately to come and propose it to me, and I'll clear the Difficulties of it; any other, but I, would enjoin you to break Company with him; but since he is extreamly proud and conceited, I am certain he would take your flight for a Defeat, and would believe your Faith to be grounded on no Reason, if you refused to hear his."

Having said so, he left me; and no sooner was his back turned, but I fell to consider attentively my Books and their Boxes, that's to say, their Covers, which seemed to me to be wonderfully Rich; the one was cut of a single Diamond, incomparably more resplendent than ours; the second looked like a prodigious great Pearl, cloven in two. My Spirit had translated those Books into the Language of that World; but because I have none of their Print, I'll now explain to you the Fashion of these two Volumes.

As I opened the Box, I found within somewhat of Metal, almost like to our

Clocks, full of I know not what little
Springs and imperceptible Engines:
It was a Book, indeed; but a Strange
and Wonderful Book, that had neither
Leaves nor Letters: In fine, it was a
Book made wholly for the Ears and
not the Eyes. So that when any Body
has a mind to read in it, he winds up
that Machine with a great many Strings;
then he turns the Hand to the Chapter
which he desires to hear, and straight,
as from the Mouth of a Man, or a Musical Instrument, proceed all the distinct
and different Sounds,[1] which the *Lunar*
Grandees make use of for expressing
their Thoughts, instead of Language.

When I since reflected on this Miraculous Invention, I no longer wondred
that the Young-Men of that Country
were more knowing at Sixteen or Eigh-
teen years Old, than the Gray-Beards
of our Climate; for knowing how to
Read as soon as Speak, they are never
without Lectures,[2] in their Chambers,

[1] Is this an anticipation of the phonograph?
[2] *Readings. Cf.* Sir Thomas Browne: "In the

their Walks, the Town, or Travelling;
they may have in their Pockets, or at
their Girdles, Thirty of these Books,
where they need but wind up a Spring
to hear a whole Chapter, and so more,
if they have a mind to hear the Book
quite through; so that you never want
the Company of all the great Men, living and Dead, who entertain you with
Living Voices. This Present employed
me about an hour; and then hanging
them to my Ears, like a pair of Pen-
dants, I went a Walking; but I was
hardly at End of the Street when I met
a Multitude of People very Melancholy.

Four of them carried upon their
Shoulders a kind of a Herse, covered
with Black: I asked a Spectator, what
that Procession, like to a Funeral in my
Country, meant? He made me answer,

that that naughty ▬▬▬, called so

by the People because of a knock he

lecture of Holy Scripture, their apprehensions are
commonly confined unto the literal sense of the
text."

had received upon the Right Knee,
being convicted of Envy and Ingrati-
tude, died the day before; and that
Twenty Years ago, the Parliament had
Condemned him to die in his Bed, and
then to be interred after his Death.
I fell a Laughing at that Answer.   And
he asking me, why?   "You amaze me,"
said I, "that that which is counted a
Blessing in our World, as a long Life,
a peaceable Death, and an Honourable
Burial, should pass here for an exem-
plary Punishment."   "What, do you
take a Burial for a precious thing then,"
replyed that Man?   "And, in good earnest, can you conceive any thing more
Horrid than a Corps crawling with
Worms, at the discretion of Toads
which feed on his Cheeks; the Plague
it self Clothed with the Body of a Man?
Good God!   The very thought of having, even when I am Dead, my Face
wrapt up in a Shroud, and a Pike-depth
of Earth upon my Mouth, makes me I
can hardly fetch breath.   The Wretch
whom you see carried here, besides the

disgrace of being thrown into a Pit, hath been Condemned to be attended by an Hundred and Fifty of his Friends; who are strictly charged, as a Punishment for their having loved an envious and ungrateful Person, to appear with a sad Countenance at his Funeral; and had it not been that the Judges took some compassion of him, imputing his Crimes partly to his want of Wit, they would have been commanded to Weep there also.

"All are Burnt here, except Malefactors: And, indeed, it is a most rational and decent Custom: For we believe, that the Fire having separated the pure from the impure, the Heat by Sympathy reassembles the natural Heat which made the Soul, and gives it force to mount up till it arrive at some Star, the Country of certain people more immaterial and intellectual than us; because their Temper ought to suit with, and participate of the Globe which they inhabit.

"However, this is not our neatest

way of Burying neither; for when any one of our Philosophers comes to an Age, wherein he finds his Wit begin to decay, and the Ice of his years to numm the Motions of his Soul, he invites all his Friends to a sumptuous Banquet; then having declared to them the Reasons that move him to bid farewel to Nature, and the little hopes he has of adding any thing more to his worthy Actions, they shew him Favour; that's to say, they suffer him to Dye; or otherwise are severe to him and command him to Live. When then, by plurality of Voices, they have put his Life into his own Hands, he acquaints his dearest Friends with the day and place. These purge, and for Four and Twenty hours abstain from Eating; then being come to the House of the Sage, and having Sacrificed to the Sun, they enter the Chamber where the generous Philosopher waits for them on a Bed of State; every one embraces him, and when it comes to his turn whom he st, having kissed him affectionately, leaning upon his Bosom, and joyning Mouth to Mouth, with his right hand he sheaths a Dagger in his Heart."

I interrupted this Discourse, saying to him that told me all, That this Manner of Acting much resembled the ways of some People of our World; and so pursued my Walk, which was so long that when I came back Dinner had been ready Two Hours. They asked me, why I came so late? It is not my Fault, said I to the Cook, who complained: I asked what it was a Clock several times in the Street, but they made me no answer but by opening their Mouths, shutting their Teeth, and turning their Faces awry.

"How," cried all the Company, "did not you know by that, that they shewed you what it was a Clock?" "Faith," said I, "they might have held their great Noses in the Sun long enough, before I had understood what they meant." "It's a Commodity," said they, "that saves them the Trouble of

a Watch; for with their Teeth they
make so true a Dial, that when they
would tell any Body the Hour of the
day, they do no more but open their
Lips, and the shadow of that Nose, falling upon their Teeth, like the Gnomon
of a Sun-Dial, makes the precise time.

" Now that you may know the reason,
why all People in this Country have
great Noses; as soon as a Woman is
brought to Bed the Midwife carries the
Child to the *Master of the Seminary;*
and exactly at the years end, the Skillful being assembled, if his Nose prove
shorter than the standing Measure,
which an Alderman keeps, he is judged
to be a *Flat Nose*, and delivered over to
be gelt.   You'l ask me, no doubt, the
Reason of that Barbarous Custom, and
how it comes to pass that we, amongst
whom Virginity is a Crime, should en-
joyn Continence by force; but know
that we do so, because after Thirty
Ages experience we have observed, that
a great Nose is the mark of a Witty,
Courteous, Affable, Generous and Lib-

eral Man; and that a little Nose is a Sign of the contrary:[1] Wherefore of *Flat Noses* we make Eunuchs, because the Republick had rather have no Children at all than Children like them."

He was still a speaking, when I saw a man come in stark Naked; I presently sat down and put on my Hat to shew him Honour, for these are the greatest Marks of Respect, that can be shew'd to any in that Country. "The Kingdom," said he, "desires you would give the Magistrates notice, before you return to your own World; because a Mathematician hath just now undertaken before the Council, that provided when you are returned home, you would make a certain Machine, that he'l teach you how to do; he'l attract your Globe, and joyn it to this."

During all this Discourse we went on

[1] *Cf.* M. Rostand's *Cyrano de Bergerac*, act I. scene iv.: "*Cyrano.* A great nose is properly the index of an affable, kindly, courteous man, witty, liberal, brave, such as I am! and such as you are forevermore precluded from supposing yourself, deplorable rogue!"

with our Dinner; and as soon as we
rose from Table, we went to take the
Air in the Garden; where taking Occasion to speak of the Generation and
Conception of things, he said to me,
"You must know, that the Earth, con-
verting it self into a Tree, from a Tree
into a Hog, and from a Hog into a
Man, is an Argument that all things
in Nature aspire to be Men; since that
is the most perfect Being, as being
a Quintessence, and the best devised
Mixture in the World; which alone
unites the Animal and Rational Life
into one.   None but a Pedant will deny
me this, when we see that a Plumb-
Tree, by the Heat of its Germ, as by a
Mouth, sucks in and digests the Earth
that's about it; that a Hog devours the
Fruit of this Tree, and converts it into
the Substance of it self; and that a
Man feeding on that Hog, reconcocts
that dead Flesh, unites it to himself,
and makes that Animal to revive under
a more Noble Species. So the Man
whom you see, perhaps threescore

years ago was no more but a Tuft of Grass in my Garden; which is the more probable, that the Opinion of the *Pythagorean Metamorphosis*, which so many Great Men maintain, in all likelyhood has only reached us to engage us into an Enquiry after the truth of it; as, in reality, we have found that Matter, and all that has a Vegetative or Sensitive Life, when once it hath attained to the period of its Perfection, wheels about again and descends into its Inanity, that it may return upon the Stage and Act the same Parts over and over." I went down extreamly satisfyed to the Garden, and was beginning to rehearse to my Companion what our Master had taught me; when the Physiognomist came to conduct us to Supper, and afterwards to Rest.

CHAPTER XVI

Of Miracles; and of Curing by the Imagination.

Next Morning, so soon as I awoke, I went to call up my Antagonist. "It is," said I, accosting him, "as great a Miracle to find a great Wit, like yours, buried in Sleep, as to see Fire without Heat and Action:" He bore with this ugly Compliment; "but," (cryed he, with a Cholerick kind of Love) "will you never leave these Fabulous Terms? Know, that these Names defame the Name of a Philosopher; and that seeing the wise Man sees nothing in the World, but what he conceives, and judges may be conceived, he ought to abhor all those Expressions of Prodigies, and extraordinary Events of Nature, which Block heads have invented to excuse the Weakness of their Understanding."

I thought my self then obliged in Conscience, to endeavour to undeceive him; and therefore, said I, "Though you be very stiff and obstinate in your Opinions, yet I have plainly seen supernatural Things happen:" "Say you so," continued he; "you little know, that the force of Imagination is able to cure all the Diseases which you attribute to supernatural Causes, by reason of a certain natural Balsam, that contains Qualities quite contrary to the qualities of the Diseases that attack us; which happens, when our Imagination informed by Pain searches in that place for the specifick Remedy, which it applies to the Poison.   That's the reason, why an able Physician of your World advises the Patient to make use of an Ignorant Doctor whom he esteems to be very knowing, rather than of a very Skilful Physician whom he may imagine to be Ignorant; because he fancies, that our Imagination labouring to recover our Health, provided it be assisted by Remedies, is able to cure us;

but that the strongest Medicines are too weak, when not applied by Imagination. Do you think it strange, that the first Men of your World lived so many Ages without the least Knowledge of Physick? No. And what might have been the Cause of that, in your judgement; unless their Nature was as yet in its force, and that natural Balsam in vigour, before they were spoilt by the Drugs wherewith Physicians consume you; it being enough then for the recovery of ones Health, earnestly to wish for it, and to imagine himself cured: So that their vigorous Fancies, plunging into that vital Oyl, extracted the Elixir of it, and applying Actives to Passives, in almost the twinkling of an Eye they found themselves as sound as before: Which, notwithstanding the Depravation of Nature, happens even at this day, though somewhat rarely; and is by the Multitude called a Miracle: For my part, I believe not a jot on't, and have this to say for my self, that it is easier for all

.these Doctors to be mistaken, than that the other may not easily come to pass: For I put the Question to them; A Patient recovered out of a Feaver, heartily desired, during his sickness, as it is like, that he might be cured, and, may be, made Vows for that effect; so that of necessity he must either have dyed, continued sick, or recovered: Had he died, then would it have been said, kind Heaven hath put an end to his Pains; Nay, and that according to his Prayers, he was now cured of all Diseases, praised be the Lord: Had his Sickness continued, one would have said, he wanted Faith; but because he is cured, it's a Miracle forsooth. Is it not far more likely, that his Fancy, being excited by violent Desires, hath done its Duty and wrought the Cure? For grant he hath escaped, what then? must it needs be a Miracle? How many have we seen, pray, and after many solemn Vows and Protestations, go to pot with all their fair Promises and Resolutions."

"But at least," replied I to him, "if

what you say of that Balsam be true, it is a mark of the Rationality of our Soul; seeing without the help of our Reason, or the Concurrence of our Will, she Acts of her self; as if being without us, she applied the Active to the Passive. Now if being separated from us she is Rational, it necessarily follows that she is Spiritual; and if you acknowledge her to be Spiritual, I conclude she is immortal; seeing Death happens to Animals, only by the changing of Forms, of which Matter alone is capable."

The Young Man at that, decently sitting down upon his Bed, and making me also to sit, discoursed, as I remember, in this manner: "As for the Soul of Beasts, which is Corporeal, I do not wonder they Die; seeing the best Harmony of the four Qualities may be dissolved, the greatest force of Blood quelled, and the loveliest Proportion of Organs disconcerted; but I wonder very much, that our intellectual, incorporeal, and immortal Soul should be con-

strained to dislodge and leave us, by
the same Cause that makes an Ox to
perish.   Hath she covenanted with
our Body, that as soon as he should receive a prick with a Sword in the Heart,
a Bullet in the Brain, or a Musket-shot
through the Chest, she should pack up
and be gone?   And if that Soul were
Spiritual, and of her self so Rational
that being separated from our Mass
she understood as well as when Clothed
with a Body; why cannot Blind Men,
born with all the fair advantages of
that intellectual Soul, imagine what it
is to see?   Is it because they are not as
yet deprived of Sight, by the Death of
all their Senses?   How!   I cannot then
make use of my Right Hand, because
I have a Left!

"And in fine, to make a just com-
parison, which will overthrow all that
you have said; I shall only alledge to
you a Painter, who cannot work without his pencil: And I'll tell you, that
it is just so with the Soul, when she
wants the use of the Senses.   Yet they'l

have the Soul, which can only act imperfectly, because of the loss of one of her Tools, in the course of Life, to be able then to work to Perfection, when after our death she hath lost them all. If they tell me, over and over again, that she needeth not these Instruments for performing her Functions, I'll tell them e'en so, That then all the Blind about the Streets ought to be Whipt at a Carts-Arse, for playing the Counterfeits in pretending not to See a bit."

He would have gone on in such impertinent Arguments, had not I stopt his Mouth, by desiring him to forbear, as he did for fear of a quarrel; for he perceived I began to be in a heat: So that he departed, and left me admiring the People of that World, amongst whom even the meanest have Naturally so much Wit; whereas those of ours have so little, and yet so dearly bought.

CHAPTER XVII.

Of the Author's Return to the Earth.

At length my Love for my Country took me off of the desire and thoughts I had of staying there; I minded nothing now but to be gone; but I saw so much impossibility in the matter, that it made me quite peevish and melancholick. My Spirit observed it, and having asked me, What was the reason that my Humor was so much altered? I frankly told him the Cause of my Melancholy; but he made me such fair Promises concerning my Return, that I relied wholly upon him. I acquainted the Council with my design; who sent for me, and made me take an Oath, that I should relate in our World, all that I had seen in that. My Pass-ports then were expeded, and my Spirit having made necessary Provisions for so long a Voyage, asked me, What part of my Country I desired to light in? I told him, that since most of the Rich Youths of *Paris,* once in their life time, made a ~~Journey to *Rome*;~~ imagining after that that there remained no more worth the doing or seeing; I prayed him to be so good as to let me imitate them.

"But withal," said I, "in what Machine shall we perform the Voyage, and what Orders do you think the Mathematician, who talked t'other day of joyning this Globe to ours, will give me?" "As to the Mathematician," said he, "let that be no hinderance to you; for he is a Man who promises much, and performs little or nothing. And as to the Machine that's to carry you back, it shall be the same which brought you to Court." "How," said I, "will the Air become as solid as the Earth, to bear your steps? I cannot believe that:" "And it is strange," replied he, "that you should believe, and not believe. Pray why should the Witches of your World, who march in the Air, and conduct whole Armies of Hail, Snow, Rain, and other Meteors, from one Province into another, have more Power than we? Pray have a little better opinion of me, than to think I would impose upon you." "The truth is," said I, "I have received so many good Offices from you, as well as *Socrates*, and the rest, for whom you have [had] so great kindness, that I dare trust my self in your hands, as now I do, resigning my self heartily up to you."

I had no sooner said the word, but he rose like a Whirl-wind, and holding me between his Arms, without the least uneasiness he made me pass that vast space which Astronomers reckon betwixt the Moon and us, in a day and a halfs time; which convinced me that they tell a Lye who say that a Millstone would be Three Hundred Threescore, and I know not how many years more, in falling from Heaven, since I was so short a while in dropping down from the Globe of the Moon upon this. At length, about the beginning of the Second day, I perceived I was drawing near our World; since I could already distinguish *Europe* from *Africa*, and both from *Asia*; when I smelt Brimstone which I saw steaming out of a very high Mountain,[1] that incommoded me so much that I fainted away upon it.

I cannot tell what befel me afterwards; but coming to my self again, I found I was amongst Briers on the side of a Hill, amidst some Shepherds, who spoke *Italian*. I knew not what was become of my Spirit, and I asked the Shepherds if they had not seen him. At that word they made the sign of the Cross, and looked upon me as if I had been a Devil my self: But when I told them that I was a Christian, and that I begg'd the Charity of them, that they would lead me to some place where I might take a little rest; they conducted me into a Village, about a Mile off; where no sooner was I come but all the Dogs of the place, from the least Cur to the biggest Mastiff, flew upon me, and had torn me to pieces, if I had not found a House wherein I saved my

[1] Vesuvius.

self: But that hindered them not to continue their Barking and Bawling, so that the Master of the House began to look upon me with an Evil Eye; and really I think, as people are very apprehensive when Accidents which they look upon to be ominous happen, that man could have delivered me up as a Prey to these accursed Beasts, had not I bethought my self that that which madded them so much at me, was the World from whence I came; because being accustomed to bark at the Moon, they smelt I was come from thence, by the scent of my Cloaths, which stuck to me as a Sea-smell hangs about those who have been long on Ship-board, for some time after they come ashore. To Air myself then, I lay three or four hours in the Sun, upon a Terrass-walk; and being afterwards come down, the Dogs, who smelt no more that influence which had made me their Enemy, left barking, and peaceably went to their several homes.

Next day I parted for *Rome*, where I saw the ruins of the Triumphs of some great men, as well as of Ages: I admired those lovely Relicks; and the Repairs of some of them made by the Modern. At length, having stayed there a fortnight in Company of *Monsieur de Cyrano* my Cousin, who advanced me Money for my Return, I went to *Civita vecchia*, and embarked in a Galley that carried me to *Marseilles*.

During all this Voyage, my mind run upon nothing but the Wonders of the last I made. At that time I began the Memoires of it; and after my return, put them into as good order, as Sickness, which confines me to Bed, would permit. But foreseeing, that it will put an end to all my Studies, and Travels;[1] that I may be as good as my word to the Council of that World; I have begg'd of *Monsieur le Bret*, my dearest and most constant Friend, that he would publish them with the History of the *Republick of the Sun*, that of the *Spark*, and some other Pieces of my Composing, if those who have Stolen

[1] Fr., "travaux," *i.e.*, old English *Travails*.

them from us restore them to him, as I earnestly adjure them to do.[1]

[1] The Manuscript of the *Bibliothèque Nationale* ends differently: "I enquired at the port when a ship would leave for France. And when I was embarked, my mind ran upon nothing but the Wonders of my Voyage. I admired a thousand times the Providence of God who had set apart these naturally Infidel men in a place by themselves where they could not corrupt his Beloved; and had punished them for their pride by abandoning them to their own self-sufficiency. Likewise I doubt not that he has put off till now the sending of any to preach the Gospel to them, for the very reason that he knew they would receive it ill; and so, hardening their hearts, it would serve but to make them deserve the harsher punishment in the world to come."

This is very likely the original ending of the work as it was circulated in Manuscript between 1649 and 1655. In any case, the particular thrust-and-parry used here is a favorite stroke with the "libertins" of the epoch in their duels against "Les Préjugés." "These are not my opinions and arguments," they say; "Heaven forbid! . . . They only express the ideas of my characters—which of course I abhor." At the same time the arguments have been stated, which was the object in view. Cyrano has several times used this method already, notably at the end of Chapter xvi.

The ending in the text above, that of all the editions, may have been substituted by Cyrano himself during his last illness.

FINIS.